James William Bowles

The world's fifth empire and other poems

James William Bowles

The world's fifth empire and other poems

ISBN/EAN: 9783337174446

Printed in Europe, USA, Canada, Australia, Japan

Cover: Foto ©Andreas Hilbeck / pixelio.de

More available books at **www.hansebooks.com**

WORLD'S FIFTH EMPIRE,

AND OTHER POEMS:

BY

JAMES WM. BOWLES.

The world is full of poetry—the air
Is living with its spirit; and the waves
Dance to the music of its melodies,
And sparkle in its brightness. Earth is veiled
And mantled with its beauty—

Percival.

LOUISVILLE, KY.
JOHN P. MORTON & Co.,
(LATE MORTON & GRISWOLD.)
1860.

JOHN P. MORTON & CO., PRINTERS, LOUISVILLE.

JOHN P. MORTON & CO., PRINTERS, LOUISVILLE.

To

NOBLE BUTLER—

A MAN EMINENT FOR ALL THOSE QUALITIES WHICH

MOST HIGHLY ADORN

THE SCHOLAR, CRITIC, PRECEPTOR, AND

GENTLEMAN,

This volume is respectfully dedicated,

BY HIS FRIEND,

The Author.

PREFACE.

His first publication the author now offers the reading world, hoping that it will look leniently upon the faults and imperfections but too evident to his own eye.

But whatever may be adjudged as to the merits of the poetical composition, the most fastidious cannot but accord commendation for the admirable manner in which the publishers—Messrs. Morton & Co., late Morton & Griswold—have performed their portion of the work. The paper is of the most excellent quality; the typography clear and beautiful, and the binding handsome and substantial. The whole execution is a powerful argument for home patronage.

The Poems presented are the productions of one who has written in his leisure hours, at various periods during the last four or five years.

He will here remark — and that explanatorily — but upon two of these,—

Firstly: " Dar-thula."   This is the versification, without the omission or interpolation of any sentiments, of a translation—by James Macpherson, Esq.,—of one of Ossian's poems, from the old Gaelic.   The author fears that the rhymic drapery he has thrown around may have somewhat concealed the strength of the features of the original; but thinks that some, perhaps, may here read this beautiful piece of composition who otherwise might never see it, and that others may prefer the versified rendering to the simple prose in which the translator has offered it to the public.

And secondly: the "Last Victim of the Deluge." To a magnificent painting by James H. Beard, Esq. of Cincinnati, the author is indebted for the title of this poem, and the principal idea upon which it is founded—that of the last survivor of the flood, a strong man—the personification of resolute and impenitent despair—sitting alone upon a rock—the only eminence above the raging seas, while all around is seen, "water, water everywhere."—All the other scenes and incidents occurring in the poem the author has drawn from a picture of the imagination.

Appreciating the salutary precept conveyed in the following quotation from "a quaint old commentator" who wrote nearly three hundred years ago,—"It hath beene the custome of many men to make their introductions to their bookes like to some Grecian Cities' gates—so ample that (as the Prouerbe ranne,) their Citie was ready to steale thorow the same;"—the author being, simply, stage-manager, and not one of the *dramatis personæ*, from the view of the spectators, will now withdraw himself behind his *paper scenes.*

Vernon, Jefferson County, Ky., May, 1860.

CONTENTS.

		PAGE.
The World's Fifth Empire, (in six cantos)		9
My Mother		111
The Harp of a Thousand Strings		118
To my Niece		121
Dar-thula		126
A Prayer for Mary		152
The Ocean Grave		154
Ode to Henry W. Longfellow, Esq.		158
Olden Memories		161
To Wm. C. Bryant, Esq.		166
The Rose		168
To the New-York Observer		176
Teedie and the Humming-Bird		178
The Vision		182
To Miss E. P.		189
The Last Victim of the Deluge		191
To C. and O.		219
To Mrs. S. A. Worthington of Cincinnati, O.		221
The Halls of Memory		226
The Captives of Babylon		230

ODE TO W. D. GALLAGHER 233
THE WHITE ANGEL 235
TO MRS. C. S. 241
ODE TO GEO. D. PRENTICE, ESQ. 244
OMNIBUS EST MORI 250
ODE TO N. P. WILLIS, ESQ. 260
TO MRS. A. C. 262
TO MRS. T. E. 264
TO MISS C. W. 267
THE STAR OF DESTINY 269
ODE TO ALFRED TENNYSON, ESQ. 280

THE POETICAL SALMAGUNDI.

PLUCK NOW THE FLOWER 285
A TRANSLATION FROM HORACE 287
TO POLLIE ANN JELICA(KE) 289
BIDDY AND PAT 291
POSSUNT QUIA POSSE VIDENTUR 293
TO MISS MERCY ELIZABETH SAMUELINA SNAGWALLADER 295
"Φίλεω τῶν Κτεανῶν" 296
AN EXAMPLE OF ALLITERATION 298
A COLLEGE SONG 299
AN ALBUMIC 302
OLD CANNIBAL VI 306
VALEDICTION 309

THE WORLD'S FIFTH EMPIRE.

CANTO FIRST.

Far o'er yon azure main thy view extend,
Where seas and skies in blue confusion blend:
Lo! there a mighty realm, by Heaven designed.
The last retreat for poor, oppressed mankind;
Formed with that pomp which marks the Hand divine,
And clothes yon vault, where worlds unnumbered shine.
Here spacious plains in solemn grandeur spread;
Here cloudy forests cast eternal shade;
Rich valleys wind the sky-tall mountains brave,
And inland seas for commerce spread the wave.
With nobler floods the sea-like rivers roll,
And fairer luster purples round the pole.

TIMOTHY DWIGHT.

THREE hundred years have flown upon time's flighty wing,

With all the woes and joys which changes ever bring;

Three hundred years have passed, have swiftly glided by,

Fleet as the lightning's flash which gilds the summer sky,

Since hidden lay a world—a mighty world unknown

Till Science headlong hurled old Error from his throne!
2

For many hundred years this land had been obscured

By Ocean's misty breath—in darkness deep immured.

Here millions of acres rich, uncultivated, wild,

Gave evidence that Eve and Adam, when beguiled

By the old Serpent's words, had sent through e'en this clime

That curse which since has walked e'er hand in hand with Time.

Here "thorns also and thistles," a bristling legion reared

Their spear-crowned heads in rank, as if they nothing feared;

Quick springing from the ground, as wild and fierce as e'en

The men, who rising up armed warriors bold were seen,

Transformed from dragon teeth, which Cadmus had sown there,

Whilst following the advice of kind Minerva fair.

Rank weeds and noxious vines tried by embrace to blind

The beaming, sparkling eye of Nature dear and kind;

O'er this great continent increasing fast were they,

Striving to bring it under their extensive sway.

But even here sweet Hope, still loving man and earth,

"On light fantastic toe," would trip along in mirth;

And every smile which fell from her bright, sunlit face

Became a gladsome flower the prospect wild to grace.

—But Hope! how came she here—kind Hope, immortal, dear?

Ah! her's a pilgrimage, long, wearisome, and drear.

When our first parents sinned, and from their Eden bright,

Their "solitary way" they took, "in lowliest plight,"

As "high in front advanced the brandished sword of God,"

Which Vengeance bore along, as quick and firm he trod,

Down, down the hill they fled " to the subjected plain,"

And casting back their eyes toward Paradise, in vain;

Terrific, awful sight! a fierce and flaming brand

Is waved o'er Eden's gate by cherub's mighty hand.

Fatigued and frightened they despairing now sink down—

The heavens grow fiercely black, then darkly on them frown.

Now paralyzed with fear, low on the ground they lie;

But Eve sees, gazing up, a bright spark in the sky—

"Oh, Adam, do behold that small but burning light,

There struggling through the gloom of this sad, woeful night,

And cleaving the rent clouds—a flaming meteor swift."

Then Adam sees it too, as his head he doth uplift.

But nearer, nearer, nearer, this light approaches them,

And glowing, sparkling, brighter than any earthly gem.

Then Adam wondering speaks to his fair, lovely Eve :

" It is an angel, dear; my eye doth not deceive."

Then coming nearer earth, it graceful circles round,

And gently as a dove, alights upon the ground.

Its snowy pinions soft, touched here and there with gold,

Approaching them with grace, now slowly doth it fold,

And kindly greeting them, thus speaks the creature fair :

" My Brother, Sister, dear, awake from grief's despair;

I am an angel sent from high Heaven down to cheer,—

My name is Hope; but trust, I always shall be near. [pleasure;

You both have sinned, you know, and roused God's just dis-

But still he did not give you stern reproof's full measure.

Down stiff, and cold, and dead, He might have stricken you ;

But this my sister Mercy prayed that He would not do.

The broad land lies before, go whither now you list;

But e'er in virtue's path I beg you to persist,

That thus somewhat you may atone for your great sin;

And Eden to regain, to strive this day begin;

For you have forfeited your loved and beauteous home,

And through this wild, strange earth, God dooms you now to roam.

But when affliction throws its shadow on your heart,
To comfort and beguile will ever be my part.
And though I e'er will love you and your children, know,
That up to Heaven again I may be forced to go;
I *may* be driven off, I *may* be grieved away;
But in behalf of you and them I sure will stay,
While there yet seems to me to be, in reason, chance,
From now till end of time, that mankind may advance,
Though slowly, e'en, and reach, at last, that high degree
Of love to God and man, which thus will make all free—
Free from transgression, sin; free from the Tempter's snare;
Free from sad misery here, and Hell's eternal glare;—
Which back will bring the world to favor and the love,
That once was given it by God who dwells above."

From that day until this, with men had Hope dwelt here,
To gild their clouds of gloom—with word and smile to cheer.
She ne'er had left the earth, though true it is that oft
She had been nearly forced to wend her way aloft.

When sea rolled high on sea, in grandeur dark and wild,

As high as Pelion great upon old Ossa piled,

And buried was the world in watery grave profound,

And hid from human eye was every spot of ground;

Hope hovered o'er the ark, and beams of light forth sent,

Which like the burnished lance the gloomy darkness rent.

And after this she roved the rough, wide world all o'er,

Living among those men whose condition she thought bore

The most resemblance to man's first estate, which he

Had lost by taking fruit from the forbidden tree.

In old Jerusalem, in Babylon the grand,

In Greece, and far-famed Rome, had lived Hope sweet and bland;

And down in later times in Britain had she stayed,

And that mankind might be free, disenthralled, had prayed.

But after dwelling there for many centuries long,

And seeing still to thrive oppression, sin, and wrong,

Unfolded she her wings torn, storm-beat, and weary,

And not contented yet, fled far the prospect dreary.

She crossed the ocean vast another land to find,

Which would encourage more her heart still unresigned;

For even Hope may pine, lament, and grieve, and sigh,
And much dispirited, long heavenward to fly.

She landed on a shore to her unknown and strange;
And o'er this new-found land she took her silent range.
She saw a people wild—a good land left to waste;
And then she hoped and prayed that God the day would haste,
When in this country fine, a better, nobler race
Than yet the earth had seen, He should think fit to place;
Or else, though loving still, she could no more here roam,
But sick and weary then would seek her heavenly home.
As only *Hope* can hope had always hoped Hope dear,
And now buoyed by this thought, she wiped her crystal tear,
And radiant grew her eye, as she resolved to be
Yet patient, and await the glorious day to see.

And thus it was, sweet Hope, still loving man and earth,
On "light fantastic toe," would trip along in mirth;
And every smile which fell from her bright sun-lit face
Became a gladsome flower the prospect wild to grace.

And mighty forests too, though beautiful and grand,
Yclad with darksome shade half this neglected land,
Which skillful husbandmen could fence, and clear, and till,
Soon making like the rose bloom every plain and hill;
While in the crowded Old World, thousands cried for bread,
Their herbage withering all before gaunt Famine's tread,
Great rivers wide and lakes their lengthy course would trace,
Divided only by the feathered or finny race,
Or by the rough canoe in which the savage fierce,
Would ply about for pleasure, or else the fish to pierce.
Here "Oniagara" rolled with thunders most profound,
And shook in its mad leap the rocks and earth around.

And were these solitudes, these plains and forests vast,
To be awakened ne'er save by the tempest's blast?
The pioneer's keen ax here never made to ring,
Where rung the savage yell, or howl of some wild thing?
Upon the throbbing bosom of river or of lake,
Would no majestic steamers their noble course here take?
And would no white man e'er cross o'er the heaving ocean,
And view that cataract, and feel that deep emotion—

That wonder, and that awe—that reverence most sublime,
Inspired by the music of Nature's grandest chime?

Oh! Skeptic, wouldst thou say no wisdom had been shown
By God in making this vast continent the throne
Of barbarism fierce—in giving it to those
Wild tribes who nothing did but hunt and war with foes?
Vain, silly worm! "God moves in a mysterious way
His wonders to perform"—wide, universal sway
Belongs to him, "he plants his foot-steps in the sea;"
The wild winds now are mute, the waves drop quietly.

The time has almost come when this great hemisphere,
Arousing from her sleep, the strenuous calls shall hear
Of Freedom, and Religion, of Science, and of Art—
Whose teachings harden mind, but soften e'er the heart.

The Old World groans beneath the chains of tyranny,
Which strive to hold and crush desire to be free—
That feeling which exists and burns in every breast,
Extinguishable ne'er, nor thus to be suppressed!

Religion's hands are tied—disgrace she there receives—
The Bible disregarded—defiled its very leaves.
Want, Hunger, Pestilence, stalk naked through the lanes,
And o'er these hapless lands old Anarchy mad reigns.

Jehovah soon will plant his foot on ocean wild,
And make it lie at rest and sleep as gentle child,—
The barrier be removed which long has lain between
The New World and the Old ;—His wisdom thus be seen.

THE WORLD'S FIFTH EMPIRE.

CANTO SECOND.

On the Genoan shore there stands a bright young boy,

Who notes with eager eye a light and tiny toy—

A little boat, which he has unassisted made,

And launched upon the gulf, in sails and flags arrayed;

And heedless of the clouds which gather dark around,

He gazes on his ship to port far distant bound.

The lightning flashing bright, the thunder threatening loud,

He thinks can never hurt his little vessel proud!

His heart throbs quick with joy—he claps his hands in glee,

As he sees her riding safe over the stormy sea.

And then a happy sailor he thinks he'll be some day,

And jump upon his ship and sail far, far away

To visit foreign lands, and see the whole, wide world;—

With cherished thoughts like these his ardent brain is whirled.

  The sapling's a small tree—a tree, the sapling large;

For like produces like, true Nature's to her charge.

And boys are little men, and men but full-grown boys;

And as the child, the youth, his thoughts and time employs,—

Though there exceptions be—when he arrives at age,

Ideas and things like these his manhood will engage.

Napoleon, when a youth, the soldier loved to play—

To lead a gallant band of his companions gay,

With onset fierce against the little fort of snow.

His future life and deeds like disposition show.

  And Hannibal, a child, when his father left for Spain,

Implored that he might go among the warlike train.

But this request refused, Hamilcar led him now
Up to an altar near, and made his son here vow,
When he became a man, to fight the Romans bold;
Which afterward he did, until worn-out and old.

And little Samuel too, who to his God was lent
By faithful Hannah good, and to old Eli sent,
Was taught by him to fear and love the Lord of all—
To minister to him, and mind Religion's call.
And after this fair child to man's estate had grown,
As faithful, zealous priest, and prophet was he known.

And nearer to our times, in our old mother-land,
There lived a youth, who oft would leave his comrade-band,
And draw with pencil skilled some plan he had designed,
Or make some small machine—by Nature thus inclined.
And when that giant mind had once become matured,
He lifted mystery's veil from things which it obscured;
And by an apple's fall he made the demonstration,
Unto the human race, of law of gravitation.

And by "Principia," and other works 'twas shown,
That he was the greatest philosopher e'er known.

And little George, the youth, was truthful, kind, and bold,
And Washington, the man—but it need not be told.
His Roman mother true, when news to her was sent,
That her loved son had been elected President,
Exhibiting no signs of great surprise or joy,
Replied, " George always was a good, obedient boy !"
Examples we might give, thus, *ad infinitum*,
Showing how often youth similar men become.
But to cite more than these would be but time ill spent;
For well 'tis known the tree grows as the shoot is bent.

We left a little boy, on an Italian shore,
Watching his gallant craft as through the waves it tore ;
And wishing he was then a man, full-grown and strong,
And o'er the billows wild was sailing swift along.

The youth became a man ; Columbus was his name—
A name now written high on the Pillar tall of Fame !

Hail Christopher Columbus!—Priests, poets, scholars, sages,

That great name still shall praise through long and future ages.

No grand ancestral line through centuries did he trace,

As far as title goes he held an humble place;

Though after glory's wreath had fallen on his brow,

There were noble families who well could *prove and vow*

That blood akin to that which gushed from his great heart,

As wild and free as streams which from the steep hills start,

Flowed through *their* princely veins—an honor which he ne'er

Did covet; for his was nobility more dear—

Nobility of heart, of character, of mind:

In what long pedigree still greater could he find?

His father, for a trade, combed wool, as we are told;

But such work did not suit the young son's spirit bold.

For Providence designed him for a nobler end,

And o'er the ocean vast 'twas fated he should wend

His way some day, and there should find a " *Golden Fleece,*"

Possession of which would man's happiness increase;

Though far more difficult it was to be obtained—

Still much more valuable when it had been gained—

Than that which Jason famed, the brave young Argonaut,
O'er waters and through lands in toils and perils sought.
His father being a man of judgment and of sense,
Perceiving the boy's love for sea was so intense,
Determined to afford him every chance he could,
That talent to develop, which well he understood.
And as it was resolved that he should go to sea,
He studied branches which most useful there would be.

When fourteen years of age—as chroniclers relate—
Led on by hand of strong, and strange, mysterious Fate,
His nautical career under the care of one
Columbo, a relative, though distant, he begun.
Of him for several years but little we are told;
But still it is enough to know that he was bold—
That he possessed a soul as wild, as strong, as free,
As e'en the billows grand which he so loved to see.

It is a cloudy morn—armed vessels lie in wait,
Near Portugal's green coast, as unsuspecting, straight,

On their fast, onward course, Venetian galleys four,

Sail o'er old Ocean's breast, all filled with golden store.

Then from their covert dark quick dart these vessels strong :—

Bellona fierce and Mars here hover all day long;

And when the curtains black of night now fall around,

Still closely grappled there, the two chief ships are found.

But Vulcan weary of the war protracted so,

Comes near, his bright red robe of fire o'er both to throw;

Which blazing wildly wraps in its extended folds

These two fine, gallant ships, and soon dominion holds.

And now into the sea the flying flame fast drives

The frightened, trembling crews, much fearing for their lives.

And those who just then strove all human life to take,

Strive human life to save, as through the waves they break.

Alas! unhappy fate—sure it is hard enough,

In a strong ship in storm to brave the billows rough ;

But thus to be there tossed by breakers rolling 'round,

With not a plank between a man and grave profound—

Yet still they struggle on, for life is dear to all,

And beat with sturdy arm the high-piled prison wall.

But Ocean, long disturbed and kept from his repose

By these stern combatants, more mad and violent grows,

Till opening his huge jaws, all foaming white with rage,

He swallows one by one, heedless of size or age;

Like Polyphemus famed—that giant Cyclops fierce—

Whose adamantine heart no human cry could pierce,

Devouring one by one shrewd Ulysses' poor band,

When driven by misfortune on the Cicilian strand.

But one still strong of heart, with arm of iron nerve,

Beats back the waves, and does not from his course yet swerve.

Yet six or eight miles long lie 'tween him and the shore;

High billows 'round him roll, wild winds above him roar.

At times it seems that he must find a watery grave;

When that strong arm grows weak what power then can save?

But He who measures seas in the hollow of his hand,

And marks the sparrow's fall, brings him at last to land.

But who this hero bold, miraculously brought

To shore, when Ocean's caves with friends and foes are fraught?

He must be destined for some grander end in life,

Than murdering fellow-men, and making war and strife.

Yes, who this hero bold?   Columbus is his name—

A name now written high on the Pillar tall of Fame.

We turn our eyes to Spain.   Now Night her sable wings

Has spread o'er hill and vale, and o'er all living things,

Whose darksome shadows tell that it is time to rest,

While Sol wraps in his clouds, and sinks down in the west.

But still there plods along, o'er Andalusia's plain,

A stranger, with a boy, on foot, who seeks to gain

A town not distant far.   His is an humble guise;

But garments such as these have often clad the wise.

Oft does an honest heart beat 'neath a pile of rags,

While villain wears broadcloth, and of his station brags.

Though tired and weary much, he still appears to bear

No lowly, common mien, but high, distinguished air.

In his capacious brain revolves a mighty scheme,

The impulse of whose rush, as on it whirls, would seem

To dash the gushing blood each swelling vein along,

As giant mill-wheel throws, with revolution strong,

Through channel worn and torn, the waters wont to spread,

And leap as if they wished to leave their natural bed.

There is another world—and this thought fills his mind—

There is another world, which he has yet to find.

But Fortune has not poured into his lap her gold,

By means of which he may perform that project bold.

In his own native land he help in vain has sought;

To Portugal's young king his humble plea's next brought;

But John refuses too that sparkling western gem,

Which might glow like a star, in his bright diadem.

And now his brother has to Albion great been sent,

To know if *she* would have the jewel he'd present.

They reach a convent now; the strange man taps the door,

And for his boy requests of food a little store.

The Prior good comes by while they are standing there,

And struck by his appearance, and knowing from his air

And accent, that the man is from a foreign land,

Addresses him some words, in manner free and bland.

He learns his name and tale, and bids him there to rest;

And at La Rabida he makes him thus his guest.

Here is the turning-point in our great hero's life.

For ridiculed and scorned, with disappointment rife,

He has determined now to leave Hispania old,

And thence to England go, whose king he has been told,

Has some attention paid to his grand plans and schemes.

His star of hope still shines, still throws on him its beams.

And thus his stopping here is made immediate cause—

For Fortune has a code of arbitrary laws,

Which she can make to suit each individual case;

And oft to place and time, a man for deeds may trace

Both being and origin; and from small circumstance,

Some great event may find, as oft it seems, from chance.

A dead and rotten tree, prostrated on the ground,

May turn aside some stream, to distant ocean bound,

From its own usual course, and making it pour o'er

Tall cliff, in time produce a cataract with roar,

And thunder loud and wild, and beauty, grandeur, all,

Of great Niagara, in its mad leap and fall!

And so in the tide of man's affairs some trifling thing,

As primary cause, a great and grand result may bring

By turning its first channel, and making it to flow—

Though passive there it lies—where, else, it ne'er would go.

But as we said before, his stopping here is made,

Thus the immediate cause—though still sometime delayed—

Of his discovery of the New World great and vast—

A brilliant, glowing page, in Time's long history past.

Juan Perez, the prior, when made to understand,

That hence his guest will seek help in some other land,

And that thus glory's wreath may grace some other brow,

Than his Hispania's dear, quick for a friend sends now—

Named Garcia Fernandez, a scientific man,

Who comes and listens well, and soon approves the plan.

And several times they meet, at this old convent, then;

And with these wise savans, a few sea-faring men,

Who great attention give to his gigantic scheme,

And of its prosecution they now in favor seem,

In high regard the prior by Isabella great

Is held; persuading now Columbus here to wait,

He writes a letter in behalf of him, his guest;

And there, in earnest tones, he pleads that the request

For help she now may grant, for her own royal crown,

Her country's interest too, and glory, and renown.

Our hero had at first, with great regret, resolved

To leave Hispania old; but in debt much involved,

He had concluded then to seek in other land

Means for the accomplishment of his dear project grand.

So, thus besought, he stays, and long time has this home,

Unwilling, vexed, and crossed, through other lands to roam,

While there seems any chance for him to ever find

Assistance to perform *the* thought of his strong mind.

Sustained by promises, for years he's made to wait;

And from a stand-point high—his elevation great,

Of intellect and soul—he views the golden prize—

This longed-for, promised land, spread out before his eyes,

As hand of Faith aside draws Ocean's misty veil,

Obscuring others' sight by its long, heavy trail—

But fearing e'er that he, like to old Moses good,

Who led by God himself, upon Mount Pisgah stood,

And viewed rich Canaan broad—would never be allowed

To place his foot thereon, and walk triumphant, proud.

  But still the longest night at last flees from the sun ;

All things have had an end, or must have, once begun ;

No path such length can have, that there's no terminus ;

E'en earth shall end, with all its woes, and strife, and fuss.

Now Isabella good, and Ferdinand her lord,

When the stern Moorish kings, by blood, and fire, and sword,

Have thus been driven out of their Alhambra grand,

Retreating slow before their firm, brave Christian band—

When in the changing heavens the crescent bright had waned,

And faded from the place which it had there maintained

For eight long centuries, now superseded by

The cross, which throws its length from zenith of the sky

To the horizon down—the Christian's beacon-light,

Marking the dawn of day, where all before was night ; —

Yes, now the sovereigns pay attention to his plea ;

And after some delay and thought they then agree

To give the aid required; though true it is, not till
Columbus left the court, determined that he still
Would not be subject to procrastination and
Such wavering promises; but to another land—
France—now would go, and try for better fortune there.
'Tis only then that they would promise to prepare,
As soon as possible, the expedition which
Was destined soon to find a new world vast and rich.

Upon the trackless sea three vessels frail are tossed,
Like weary, sea-worn birds which far their course have lost.
The crews disheartened seem, save one undaunted soul,
Who there majestic stands, as billows round him roll!
For many, many weeks those ships have sailed the deep,
Where nothing else, before, save wild winds, had full sweep.
But superstitious fears, and terrors great now hold
The sailors' minds and hearts; and e'en one captain bold,
Losing his confidence, himself, would too persuade
The Admiral to turn back, ere chance of life should fade;
While many of his crew him overboard would throw,
If they but durst, and then would homeward turn and go.

The crisis-hour has come; — did so much e'er depend

Upon one single mind? — will it 'neath such weight bend?

What Dionysius' sword, o'er Damocles' head hung,

While at a banquet rich, by one hair, naked strung,

When it's compared to that responsibility,

Impending, threatening thus to crush him to the sea!

Hope, on her snowy wing, mounts high into the air,

And hovers there, almost in absolute despair.

And long she watches these white wavering barks which seem

Near land, then farther off, like phantoms in a dream!

She only hesitates until the die is cast,

And if, unfavorably, her life on earth is past;

For high above the world, the gates of Heaven are ope,

And sister-spirits call, to them, the angel Hope!

Upon Britannia's shore Religion bends her knee,

Her white robes flowing 'round, like snow-drifts, light and fre

But spotted here and there, by foul pollution's touch,

Their maiden purity, alas! thus lessened much.

Her eye as deep and blue as sea she seems to raise,
And clasps her hands in prayer, as lip her heart obeys.

And Liberty, e'en *now* in stars and stripes arrayed,
As if to typify the dress which would be made,
And given her, fore'er, by freemen great and true,—
Her hands by tyrants chained, the worst that they can do —
Walks sadly up and down old Europe's western shore,
While wistful eye she casts the throbbing sea all o'er.
For well "the mountain nymph" knows, if she cannot found
An empire in the west, she will thus e'er be bound.

And even, "there is silence in Heaven about the space
Of half an hour," but Time does not with finger trace
His hours on crystal dial, as here he e'er has done,
For there eternity has scarcely yet begun;
And to Jehovah, Lord, one day 's a thousand years,
And e'en a century long but one short day appears.
The bright, celestial beings gaze down upon the sea,
So anxious all, save God, not knowing what will be;

For deep in depths of his "unfathomable mines
Of never failing skill," he hides his "bright designs."

The angel who records — e'er ready thus to heed,
When benefactors of our race some glorious deed,
Some noble act perform — stands there with open book,
And golden pen in hand, while oft his eye doth look
To see what he shall write, the moment it is done,
Ere one more grain of sand from man's hour-glass may run.

Upon the trackless deep three vessels frail are tossed
Like weary, sea-worn birds which far their course have lost;
Their crews disheartened seem, save one undaunted soul,
Who there majestic stands, as billows round him roll!
Hark! "Land ahead! land ho!" the watchman loudly cries;
All eager catch his words and strain their longing eyes.
The mystery great is solved, his theory great is true.
To Lord of lands and seas a cross appears in view;
They dedicate a world to Him who brought them o'er,
And caused them here to land upon this golden shore.

The world's a mighty stage, and all men actors there,—
'Tis said—the rich, the poor, the old, the young, the fair.
Some few conspicuous stand, but most the background hold;
Not all these low and mean, not all those great and bold.
But how oft, when a man has glory's fair wreath won,
And Conscience whispers soft, in such one's ear, "Well done,
Thou good and faithful servant," and great and prominent
He stands, with this reward now happy and content,
That those whose thoughts and instincts fit them for menial place,
By arts, deceit, and craft, will try such to debase,
By dragging him back from his proud position high,
And striving hard to make him in *their* lowness lie!

In this our drama now, again the scenes we shift,
And curtains of the past, on this new act we lift.
'Tis in a southern clime, and in a beauteous isle,—
Though winter, Nature here seems mildly yet to smile—
One of a cluster green, which glows 'neath tropic light,
On Ocean's throbbing breast—a string of emeralds bright.

Now San Domingo's streets seem all alive in motion,

Solemn, sublime, and deep, as that of grand old Ocean!

A long procession slow—a funeral march is seen;

Oh! who has left earth's stage—some mighty king or queen?

' Midst ceremony great, and pomp, and show, parade,

' Midst banners wrapped in crape, a coffin is conveyed

Down to a ship in port, while friars their low chants sing,

And with artillery's boom the air is made to ring.

Ah! could those bones, that dust, borne there by persons great

Of various orders all, composing church and state,

Again rise into life,—as once arose at Nain

The widow's only son, addressing all his train—

What words would those around, who honored him, now hear,

As resurrected he would speak from his black bier?

"Ah! commentary strange upon this human life,

With its neglect, and shame, and pride, and pomp, and strife.

Three hundred years ago, here I was thrown in chains,

In stern corporeal woes, in cruel mental pains,

By one who claimed that he had his commission got,

From Ferdinand, my king—ah! black, eternal spot

Upon *his* character; for though, when I had come

Unto his court, he vowed that it was done by some

Unwarrantable power which he ne'er meant to give,

Still long and many years, in his sight did I live,

And dispossessed of all which I aforetime held,

Till all my brilliant hopes, like bubbles, were dispelled.

Thought he, my rising sun of fame with its bright blaze

Would soon eclipse, fore'er, his diadem's bright rays?

I, who had broken down those barriers strong between

The two great hemispheres, and also first land seen;—

Yes, I, who thus had found such lands as these, and then

Had added them unto the Spanish realm, by men

Was superseded thus, and thought not fit as they

To hold, in my king's name, o'er one square foot the sway!

By men, who grasped for power, and tried to take from me,

What they could never *win*, through all eternity.

Was this then my reward?—was I thus to be hurled,

In dark oblivion's grave, because I found a world?

"Ah! thou mean Selfishness! man's little household god,

At whose well-understood, exacting, frequent nod,

He bends his abject knee; — an idol for whose stand

He has carved out a block from heart of stone hard, and

Exalting which he notes its jealous, *downcast* eye

Which can see none, save those who at its feet slaves lie.

And then in niches 'round this god he oft will place

Figures of Envy and Ingratitude most base,

And Malice too, and Hate, all watchful e'er to see —

As body-guard — safe his supreme divinity!

Unfortunate the man whose flitting shadow e'er

May fall 'tween him and these *penates* loved and dear!

"Why e'en another's name is given to the realm

Toward which I first did turn my bold, unswerving helm;

And but for poets ne'er would the strange uncommon word,

'Columbia'— and then but to *half* applied — be heard!

But true it seems that you would reverence now my name,

Would honor too my bones, acknowledging my fame ;

Yet still take heed lest there should be some, too, 'mong you,

To whom you do not give the honor that is due.

"You take my bones and dust to old Havana, where
They will be placed with pomp, parade, and show, and care;
But needless then to raise for me a pillar high,
By which you may exalt my name unto the sky;
For I've, like Horace old, built my own monument
Which through the ages long my fame shall there present;
And neither floods, nor winds, nor gnawing tooth of Time,
Shall ever there erase that name and fame sublime!

"I leave the world again, and that without regret,
For why wish here to live, and suffer, toil and fret,
Where Pseudo-Merit sits supreme upon the throne,
From which true Worth has been thus, *vi et armis*, torn?
Go study well my fate—remember what I tell;
But now I leave this life, and bid you all farewell!"

How true! and was it not a commentary strange
Upon this human life, with all its fleeting change?
That body which had been, three hundred years before,
Borne from that very port, bending, and suffering sore

'Neath ignominious irons, and stern Misfortune's frown,

With honors such as these, to-day, is loaded down !

And true, another's name was given to the world,

In which the Spanish flag Columbus first unfurled;

The bearer of which name, it's been asserted long,

Most probably ne'er made the voyage on which strong

Claims he himself had laid unto this honor great,

And too successfully—oh ! strange caprice of Fate !

E'en if our hero was not first to see main-land,

It matters little quite, for his own project grand

Had been performed in spite of opposition all ;

His theory great was proved ; the strong old Chinese wall,

Between two worlds, had been thus broken down, and then

The breach which he had made was entered but by men,

Who following in his track, and stealing his great fame,

Might take it, each to gild and polish his own name.

But be it told, for true, a century long before

The good, old ship, May-flower, touched this bright western shore,

The name was given it, and names like habits old,

And ancient customs too, cannot e'er be controlled,

And changed at pleasure, e'en when they should be, of right;

In long habitual use there is such power and might.

But though another's name was given to the whole,

(Although his chariot wheels did not first reach the goal,

If e'er they reached at all, but only—for we may

Afford to grant this so—just following in the way

Marked plainly out for him, went farther on than those

Of his competitor's whose claims he did oppose,)

Yet still a score of parts of this great hemisphere

Is called by name of him, who really first stood here,—

A name the good, the great, the just, the learned, the wise

Of all enlightened lands beneath the azure skies,

Unite to honor now.

      How true, no prophet is

Without renown and fame in any land save his:

And oh! how oft it is men fail to recognise

Real merit shining plain before their very eyes!

And mankind, scarcely e'er, seem to appreciate

Goodness and greatness of the truly good and great,

In times in which they live;—and not till future ages,

Often, are they adjudged, heroes, and saints, and sages.

But struggle nobly on, thou benefactor of

Thy fellow-man, and feel, to gain respect and love

E'en of posterity, and the approving smile

Of Conscience and of Heaven just recompense; nor guile,

Nor malice, nor envy fear, of any jealous foe; —

For verily, thou shalt have thy due reward,—this know.

THE WORLD'S FIFTH EMPIRE.

CANTO THIRD.

Still one great clime, in full and free defiance,
Yet rears her crest, unconquered and sublime,
Above the far Atlantic !   She has taught
Her Esau brethren that the haughty flag,
The floating fence of Albion's feebler crag,
May strike to those whose red right hands have bought
Rights cheaply earned with blood.

BYRON'S ODE.

Let the bloody flag be furled,
  Nobler is the task we're set,
And 'tis treason to the world
  To neglect it, or forget.
Science woos us to her arms ;
  New discovery waits our time ;
Young invention speads her charms ;
  Knowledge beckons us to climb ;
Brothers, join us in the van,
And we'll lead the march of man.

CHARLES MACKAY.
"A Remonstrance with the Americans."

Two hundred years have flown upon Time's flighty wing,

With all the woes and joys which changes ever bring ;

Two hundred years have past, have swiftly glided by,

Fleet as the lightning's flash which gilds the summer sky,

Since o'er the heaving bosom of Ocean wild and vast

A white may-flower was borne by old Æolus' blast.

That blossom fair but frail on Columbia's shore was thrown;

It withered and decayed, but soon its seeds were grown.

And now the course of empire far westward takes its way;

And open lies the Bible, and dawns a brighter day.

The Pilgrims think that they, their children and their land,

Will evermore be free from hard oppression's hand;

'Twas persecution's lash, which drove them o'er the sea—

Conscience and Liberty, each bids them thus be free.

' Tis true they have afflictions, privations, toils, and woes;

But strong in heart and hand they conquer all such foes.

'Tis true, with Indians fierce they often must contend;

But then against these tribes themselves they can defend.

They labors such and trials prefer to tyrant's rod

Which long prevented them from worshiping their God.

They live, and work, and toil; then pass off, one by one,

Not fearing to meet death, conscious of duty done.

Their sons inherit all the virtues of their sires,

And in their manly breasts burn Liberty's bright fires.

They have been taught to fear one true and mighty God,
But not to bow down at a human despot's nod.
To worship as they pleased their fathers good came here,
Themselves also to govern, no other lords to fear.
Such sentiments, as these, spring in their breasts innate,
And is it strange that they should tyranny thus hate?

A rich, broad land they have ; religious freedom's theirs,
And civil, too, oh! should they entertain e'er fears,
That they will be disturbed in the possession of
These privileges sweet, now Heaven's so bright above?
An ocean rolls between the New World and the Old,
They think themselves secure behind this barrier bold.

How like an April morn, when Phœbus brightly smiles!
The farmer views the skies, and dreams not he of wiles.
He plows his fertile land, prepares his seed to sow,
When thunder rolls above, and winds begin to blow.
For slowly o'er the sea, there moves a threatening cloud ;
Upon it figures strange inscribed by tyrants proud ;

But as it nearer draws, distinct those letters seem,

"Chains or Death, Death or Chains!" such words there

    fiercely gleam.

Long hung that cloud above, that cloud so dark and frowning,

True Freedom's mountain-peaks, thus like a death-cap crowning!

A firm answer gave the child to her cruel mother proud:

"Oh! give me liberty, or wrap me in a shroud!"

Then bursts forth the war-storm, amid artillery's thunder.

The world looks on the strife in mingled hope and wonder.

But in the mother-land, oh! are they none who dare

To cry against such wrong, though hundreds at them stare,

And on their noble heads cast deep reproach and shame,

And for Columbia's acts, e'en vow they are to blame,

And call all such fell foes to their beloved land,

Because for Freedom's sake they take a noble stand?

And when she now remonstrates against her unjust laws,

Oh! are there none to speak for Right's and Truth's dear cause?

Yes, God be praised, there are, a few, a manly few,

Who plead with tongues of fire for all that's right and true!

Yes, Barré, Freedom's lover, great Barré first stands there,

His gallant arm to raise for our Columbia fair.

Useless for foes to say, that she, and every son

Owed gratitude for acts of kindness, favor done

By Britain mild and good;—that England sowed the seed,

And pruned and reared the tree, and cut down every weed.

"They planted by your care!   Oppression planted them.

They fleeing from your rod dared ocean's perils stem.

Unto a barren country the driven pilgrims went,

Where trials and sufferings sore, and hardships Fortune sent,

Such as humanity is scarce e'er called to bear;

And among many others which I might mention, were

Cruelties and terrors of a fierce, and savage foe,

The most formidable, which God's whole earth doth know!

But still with English liberty bright burning in their breast,

They chose thus to be cursed, rather than by you *blessed.*

Reared by your indulgence!   They grew by your *neglect.*

When you began to *care* for them their growth was checked.

That care was exercised, in sending persons there

To rule them, and to spy, to make their actions wear

The aspect of rebellion ;—yes, men whose deeds, I know,

Have oft-times made the blood cease freely on to flow

Along the veins of these bold Sons of Liberty ;—

Yes, men too glad to go, from justice here to flee.

Protected by your arms ! They have defended *you.*

For they have taken arms duty to *your* land to do.

Amid their labors hard, great valor have they used

There to defend a country, whose frontier was suffused

With their own blood ; while its interior parts did yield

Its savings for your coffers ; — thus you did they shield.

"And these people, I believe, are loyal subjects true,

But jealous of their liberties, as dear to them as you ;

And ready at any time, should you offend their right,

To rise in majesty, and for their freedom fight ! "

And William Pitt is there, the good, the noble, great :

"You say, our Colonies are rebels obstinate.

And that they *have* resisted I heartily rejoice.

Three millions all so deaf to Liberty's strong voice,

As to submit like slaves, when still they might be free,

But to enslave the others fit instruments would be.

America, you say, is weak, but Britain strong ;

'Tis true in a good cause, but not when in the wrong,

Our country great might crush this young colonial land,

But against injustice such I will e'er lift my hand.

In such an unjust cause, chance of success were small ;

And if indeed she fell, like the strong man would she fall ;

Embracing, in tight grasp, the pillars of the State,

With her downfall would fall our Constitution great ! "

Burke, greatest orator of all, is there, and tries

With noblest eloquence to open the dull eyes

Of his own countrymen, who blindly forward rush

Vowing 'neath their legions' feet Freedom's sons to crush!

These for Columbia fight, along with a few others,

Though overborne by thousands,— a band of Theban brothers,

Whose names with Lafayette's forever linked should be,

Champions of Right and Truth, dear friends of Liberty !

But, Lafayette! Oh who can mention thy loved name,

Resounding 'mong Time's hills, sounded by trump of Fame,

And not one moment stop, a tribute small to pay

Of veneration, love?— Oh! who could not long stay,

And on thy statue gaze, which the great artist skilled

Has from his marble cut, with life, soul, vigor filled,—

Almost as natural form, as sprung from each rough stone,

Which o'er the head of Pyrrha and old Deucalion, thrown,

Became a living man, who saw, and felt, and talked,

And conscious of real life, in noble manhood walked?

Who thoughtful, standing there, and gazing could not see,

That eye grow bright, and flash with fire of liberty?

Who musing could not see blood mantling to that cheek,

And those lips quiver quick, as if they wished to speak

A word for FREEDOM's cause,—not see uplifted arm

Thrill with new strength, as if to shield her from all harm,—

Not see that noble heart, beat 'gainst its marble wall,

As if it still were moved by her inspiring call,—

Not stand and gaze thereon, until that figure grows

Twin to the image dear, which his heart holds, and knows!

And Kosciusko, too! oh! no we'll not neglect
To speak a word for him —a token of respect.
At mention of that name, a bright, electric spark —
Glowing like the comet's, amid surrounding dark —
Of warm enthusiasm; of pleasure, and of joy,
E'en in the coldest soul, should speedily destroy
All lethargy of regard and feeling toward his land,
And kindle smouldering fires of patriotism, fanned
By fluttering of the wings of thoughts horoic, strong,
Awakening country's love, as through his mind they throng.

Why Arnold, e'en, accursed,—before his last step fell
Which led him to the brink of a foul traitor's hell—
Why e'en a man thus sunk in degradation's mire,
It seems the very sound of such names might inspire
With nobler resolves still, and make him then retrace
His black, polluted path, and upward throw his face,
To catch the glorious beams of Liberty's bright sun,
And not, like some poor owl, turn off his head to shun!

"Oh! give me liberty, or wrap me in a shroud!"
Exclaims Columbia fair.   Then breaks that threatening cloud,
And forth the war-storm bursts amid artillery's thunder!
The world looks on the strife in mingled hope and wonder.
The kings and queens of earth with Albion sympathise,
The *people*, for the child, turn heavenward hearts and eyes.
Herostrātus, the Greek, once caused a temple's flame—
Thus to immortalize him—on skies to brand his name.
Ah! England wouldst thou fire dear Freedom's temple grand,
And on Columbia's sky they name and shame thus brand !
For fire and rapine, murder, thy armies these attend;
But WASHINGTON is there, his country to defend.

Hark! muffle now your drums, ye foes of freeman brave,
In yon lone grove the chief prays God his land to save;
Submits the cause to him, and begs his blessing now,
While light from Heaven's gate half open gilds his brow !
He feels his prayer is heard, then mounts his eager steed—
With what assurance now his army doth he lead !
A cloud guides him by day, a fiery pillar, night ;
Hope with her voice cheers him, and God's controls the fight,

But WASHINGTON!—oh! had I now a tongue of fire,
Like some great seraph high, to speak thoughts which inspire
The patriot's burning heart, when power in that loved name,
A magic strength unseen, so like, though not the same
As electricity's invincible, hidden, strong,
Which in its latent might, a genius moves along!—
When power in that loved name o'erwhelms his ardent soul,
And through its channels full makes gratitude's streams roll
Too deep for utterance, as through the giant veins
Of Terra waters flow, not with loud, noisy strains,
But rivers silent, grand, strong, fathomless, and clear,
While only babbling brooks break forth and strike the ear!

But on this HERO true, no eulogy we speak;
We no encomium give — such an attempt were weak.
Nor will we his great deeds presume here to record;—
The world his actions know, his fame as earth is broad.

'Tis said that he a youth, once up the Natural Bridge,
In peril, fearless climbed clinging to ledge and ridge;

And there engraved his name upon a giant block,

By nature's Architect laid firm — a solid rock —

So high that greatest flood, when swollen it would tear

Along, could never reach, and out those letters wear.

On an adamantine wall of a stupendous cliff,

And higher than Atlas far, or " towering Teneriffe,"

Supporting the universe in glorious strength sublime,—

Founded on endless space — the pyramid of time —

Fame with her chisel has that mighty name cut deep,

And great eternity's strong waves, as by they sweep,

May never wash away those characters of light,

Placed not too high for man's, nor low for angel's sight !

But here, my countrymen, with deep emotion now

I you congratulate, while grateful heart I bow

To Him who ever led the "Father of his Land,"

Along his pathway here, so kindly by the hand —

That *you yourselves possess the crumbling bones and dust*

Cf him you love—of all earth the greatest and most just.

The house wherein he lived, the ground whereon he trod,

Doth to you also belong ;— return thanks to your God.

But say, what earthly one should you for this most praise?

To what great patriot true should grateful hearts now raise

A national, rich song, expressing what they feel

Toward benefactor such, working for public weal,

And to do honor some and justice to one dear,

Whose memory is so sweet to freemen far and near?   [name

"Great EVERETT! good EVERETT!" millions of tongues that

In raptures wild repeat,—"In the temple grand of Fame

We'll place his statue, too, of purest marble, which

Shall stand by Washington's, high in conspicuous niche!—

An orator as great as any beneath the sun,

A man who in each trust has his full duty done.

No *politician*, he the statesman, patriot, stands—

Deep foot-prints will he leave upon Time's golden sands!"

But from digression long 'tis time we should return,

Though these themes make our hearts with love's bright beams

    to burn.

We left Columbia's sons and Albion's in war fierce,

E'er watching Freedom's life, e'er trying her to pierce.

6

But as from Sinai's top, 'mid thunders, lightnings bright,

Those rolling hoarsely 'round, these gilding with their light,

While o'er the lofty peak, hung heavy a thick cloud,

All Israel trembling much at trump "exceeding loud,"

God uttered forth the just and holy decade-law,

Adapted for mankind, without one single flaw;

So on Columbia's hills amid a mighty storm,

In the great firmament political, a form,

In mystery had appeared,—Herald of Liberty —

And sounding bugle clear, had bid her sons be free;

And loud as Stentor old, there given to the world,

As flag of stars and stripes, he o'er his head unfurled,

The Declaration great of Independence, whose

Reverberations wild will ne'er their echoes lose,

'Mong crags and vales and plains, where shall beat hearts of steel,

While man is *man*, and feels as freeman true *should* feel!

Impossible it is to conquer men like these,

Though easy quite it be, to harass, vex, and tease.

For eight years long they fight, as none but freemen fight;

Successful generally, but sometimes in sad plight.

Yes, though the eagle swift of victory perched upon
Their flag the greatest while—still ever and anon,
Like bird of omen ill, frowning Defeat would fly,
As if God chastened them, athwart the freemen's sky,
And with the shadow dark — as with a cloud of gloom —
Of her black wing would hold—like tapers in a tomb—
The glowing, sparkling beams of Liberty's bright sun,
And for a while perhaps their burning hopes thus stun!
Ah! more than once a grave in the forest's lonely glade,
By bright British bayonets, for Freedom true, was made;
But with the shield of truth she warded each strong blow,
Impenetrable e'en as the buckler which once low
From the heavens fell in Rome, while the oracle declared
That its possessors should from death, defeat be spared
So long as it they held, and conquering every land,
As rulers of the world in pride and glory stand!

Now young Columbia's foes outdone despondent grew,
Seeing her hopeful still, invincible and true.
Acknowledging at last her independent, free,
Returned they to their homes across the broad, deep sea.

And then the war-storm ceased, the contest fierce was o'er,
And heartfelt shouts of joy arose from shore to shore.
And Liberty's great sun shone brighter than it e'er
Had done since earth began — no cloud was longer near.
The eagle upward soared, and flashed like fire his eye,
As guarding sea and land, he spread his wings on high.

Our fathers ne'er were slaves; no, they were freemen born,
Back Britain's chains they hurled with wrath, indignant scorn.
Her great triumphal car they never drew along,
As foreign captives drew old Cæsar's chariot strong.
Their proud and stubborn necks a yoke could never bear,
And slavery's manacles their hands could never wear!

With all their changes years now swift away had passed
And young Columbia fair in power and strength grown fast,
When Albion jealous grew of her proud stand and fame,
And tried from earth to blot her great and honored name.
Upon the mighty ocean they grasped in deadly fight;
Then Albion's glory sunk in deepest, darkest night!

But though that mother proud, and brave, but envied child

Once drew each other's flood, long they've been reconciled.

And henceforth let each show, a great and glorious nation,

Of other's virtues all a nobler appreciation.

For if upon this earth there be two mighty states,

Where Truth o'er Sin and Error ever predominates;

Where Liberty is loved—"*vox populi*" the cry,

These Christian lands are they, none others 'neath the sky.

Britannia let us love next to Columbia dear,

Her glorious name and fame e'er cherish and revere.

She always ready is to take us by the hand,

Humanity's great cause to give a solid stand!—

To patronize with us literature, science, art,

Developing best qualities of intellect and heart.

Upon the ocean deep, throughout the entire world,

Our banners are respected, where'er they are unfurled.

Thus 'neath protection joint, Religion keeps her throne,

And thus in every land her precious seeds are sown.

Soon may these hearts whose throb is felt in every clime,

Forever be united in unison sublime;

And then may each one's active, powerful pulsation,

Meet with a quick response in similar vibration !

THE WORLD'S FIFTH EMPIRE.

CANTO FOURTH.

Columbia, Columbia, to glory arise,
The queen of the world, and the child of the skies.
     *   *   *   *
Thy reign is the last, and the noblest of time;
Most fruitful thy soil, most inviting thy clime.
     *   *   *   *
On freedom's broad basis that empire shall rise,
Extend with the main, and dissolve with the skes.
Fair Science her gates to thy sons shall unbar,
And the east see thy morn hide the beams of her star.
     *   *   *   *
To thee, the last refuge of virtue designed,
Shall fly from all nations the best of mankind.

DWIGHT.

Thou shalt be blessed above all people.

DEUT. VII 14.

"Oh! woodman, spare that tree!" the youth cries in his grief,

"My father placed it there, oh! touch not e'en a leaf!"

From Hyacinthus' blood a flower once reared its head;

Sprung the tree of Liberty from patriots' life-blood red!

Old Europe's mightiest power twice tried to fell that tree,

But all her efforts failed, and sank beneath Time's sea.

Thus warning let all take, nor touch with ax its roots.

Our fathers placed it there, and trained with pride its shoots.

It rears aloft its head, and stretches wide its arms;

Bids Freedom's lovers find a refuge from all harms.

And men of every nation beneath its shade can rest,

And safely there enjoy our fathers' good bequest.

'Tis false, "man never is, but always *to be*, blest;"

Howe'er we may respect the man, who this expressed.

The blessings of our race lie not far off concealed

Behind the future's veil, but to us are revealed.

Abstractions not are they, but real and seen and felt,

As visible as manna, when God 'mong Israel dwelt,

Which from the skies would fall, and cover all the ground,

And cause the barren sand with plenty to abound.

Thus here God showers his gifts, and makes his grace descend,

Like dews, as if he wished both earth and Heaven to blend

In a silvery flood of love, through medium which the soul,

As the eagle mounts the air, may reach its shining goal.

When follow *we* the smile of Hope's face radiant, bright,

It never us deceives as an *ignis fatuus'* light.

Oh! if the privilege to worship as we please,

No union, church with state, whose shadow cold might freeze,

Or darken somewhat the streams of veneration, love,

Which never should be checked once touched by finger of

Jehovah, Lord of all, as pure, as bright, as free,

While flowing on unto Eternity's wide sea,

E'en as those waters sprung from rock struck by the rod

Of Moses with power none, save simply faith in God;—

Oh! if the privilege we have to make our laws,

And make such laws as we think will subserve the cause

Of justice and of right,—and men alone to choose,

Whom we would wish to rule, all others to refuse;—

If privileges such, which long we have possessed,

Are not especial blessings, then true, we are not blessed.

And if to have a land embraced by every zone,

With every kind of climate, which unto us is known,

Girdled by belt of ice, or there by chain of fire;

Here by warm bands or cool, which moderate doth inspire

A pleasant temperature into the air around,

Making delightful breeze thus ever to abound;

And then on either side, as up or down we go,

Approaching by degrees to land of flame or snow ;—

Yes, if to have a land, within whose great domain,

At different seasons grow all kinds of fruit and grain,

Such as most other nations must seek the wide world o'er,

If they should wish to find, and visit many a shore ;—

Yes, if to have a land, dearer to us by far,

Because 'twas bought by toils, and labors, blood, and war;

Where gold and silver, iron, and lead and coal and stone,

Within her fruitful womb are to perfection grown ;—

If having such a land as long we have possessed,

Is not a mighty blessing, then, true, we are not blessed.

And if to live within the borders of a land,

Where twice ten thousand temples of God in beauty stand,

And point with graceful spires up toward the azure sky,

Like the finger true of Faith, to turn our eyes on high ;—

Where a Christian army, in strong and bold phalanx

Of millions e'er march on, with firm and solid ranks,

Unfurling to the winds their banners white of peace,

And with the roll of drum, recruiting to increase;

Each one wearing his cross, a badge of honor, dear,

Armed with the sword of faith, which quivers not with fear;

With breast-plate strong of truth, his bosom to protect,

E'er marching with firm step, with noble head erect;—

Where Learning's temples rise on almost every hill,

And streams of Knowledge flow our country great to fill,

Each a "Pierean spring," a fount whence all may drink,

Without a price or money, and muse and study, think;—

Yes, if to live within the borders of a land,

Where e'er inventions useful, and beautiful, and grand,

Are nearer than elsewhere unto perfection brought;—

Where science, arts, religion, are to her children taught;

Where thirty million men, or more perhaps, now dwell,

The most enlightened race of which the earth can tell;—

If having all these boons, which long we have possessed,

Is not what's being blessed, then, true, we are not blessed!

Why since the day that Terra, who till that hour unborn,

Had lain in Chaos' womb,—since that great, glorious morn

When "without form, and void," she lay while Darkness frowned,

And God's bright Spirit moved the water's face around,

And loud as thunder spake a voice, "Let there be light!"

And light arose where but a moment since was night,

While all the morning stars sang loud together in glee,

And all the sons of God there shouted for joy to see

Another world come forth to manifest the power

Of Him who had done all in one short little hour!—

Yes, since old Terra's birth, and man's creation strange,

Placed in that garden fair in happiness to range,

Two greater blessings only have fallen on mankind,

Than that which was bestowed, when 'cross the sea to find

Unto the golden Indies a nearer and better course,

Sailed Christopher Columbus, and thereby found the source

Whence since have flowed such boons invaluable and grand,—

Than his discovery of this vast and glorious land!

Yes, have two greater blessings, but only two been sent,

Though many *less* have come in palace, and hut, and tent,

With their sweet smile to cheer, like angels from the skies,

And make man's heart to beat with rapture and surprise.

And first:—When man in sin's fount of pollution dire

Had steeped his very soul, and seemed thus ne'er to tire,

Unmindful of the flood, which centuries long before

Had swept the human race from every rock and shore,

And in a council solemn in Heaven's great high courts held,

Christ, glorious Son of God, by love of man impelled,

Arose and thus addressed the Father upon his throne,

Around whose august presence thin rainbow clouds were strown,

Lest angels standing near, soon blinded by the light

Of his great majesty, should sink in endless night!

"True, Father, man has sinned, and fallen from thy grace,

And thus debased thine image marked strong upon his face;

But let us mercy have on him, a poor worm frail,

Though he transgress and err, and in his duty fail.

Oh! in thy wrath provoked and indignation just,

Down in perdition's depth I pray thee not to thrust

This race which thou hast made, but send thine only Son

To that dark, sinful world to speak to every one,

And lead him back to thee; though I should suffer much,

I'll go for such a cause, to give thee glory such!"—

Yes, when upon this earth the glorious Son of God
Rode, not like human conqueror bearing his sword and rod,
And in a chariot gilt, with dazzling pomp, parade,
As if the whole wide world was for his glory made,
But seated upon an ass, and lowly thus appeared,
And though a royal Prince by humble parents reared,—
A greater blessing this—such mercy, grace, and love!
Ah! yes the greatest far that e'er came from above.

Thence many hundred years, when Terra had been chained
Firm to a column of the empire o'er which reigned,
As sovereign lord and king, Satan, "by merit raised
To that bad eminence," by demons feared and praised—
Chained with fetters ponderous, and sunk in clouds of gloom,
While vultures of darkness sat by ever to consume
Her throbbing, bleeding heart; (like to Prometheus bound
To a pillar of the hills by Jove, while him around
All night an eagle flew—e'en more insatiate
Than were the harpies famed—impatient quite to wait
Till daylight should appear, when his poor liver torn
Should give another feast, then to its full size grown—

Bound thus till Hercules had broken his bonds strong,

And killed the bird which had tormented him so long)

Chained with fetters ponderous, till Luther in his might

Had grasped and crushed them all, and led her from the night;

Thence many hundred years, when Terra in sins dead

Was roused by a mighty voice, which in loud thunders said :

" Rise! fallen child of God, rise from thy dreary tomb,

Thou must be born again, shake off that shroud of gloom ;"—

And when inquiring if she really must indeed

Enter old Chaos' womb, and there lie still till freed

By second birth, the voice replied distinct and clear,

" Thou must be born of water and of the Spirit, hear ! "—

As unto Nicodemus, Christ teaching once spake, and

Thus made this master old of Israel understand

The difference great between the spirit and the flesh ;

And how, when man's soul had been caught in sin's strong mesh,

It must be born again, receive another shape,

Before from this tight net it e'er can make escape;—

When Terra was re-born, created then anew,

A greater blessing this, greater perhaps, 'tis true.

But save these blessings rich, Christ's mission here on earth,

And Terra's wonderful and glorious second birth,

None other greater has e'er fallen on mankind

Than that which was bestowed, when 'cross the sea to find,

Unto the golden Indies, a better and nearer course,

Sailed Christopher Columbus and thereby found the source,

Whence since have flowed such boons invaluable and grand,—

Than his discovery of this vast and glorious land.

If having such a land as long we have possessed

Is not what's being blessed, then true we *are not* blessed !

Columbia ! loved Columbia ! thou home of patriots true,

The *mention* of thy name will e'er our love renew !

Accept the grateful homage a grateful people give,

As long as time shall be, while Liberty shall live.

Thou land of hills and valleys, where towering mountains rise,

And rear their snow-wreathed brows high upward to the skies !

Thou land of plains and forests where mighty rivers roll

Along thy healthy veins far onward to their goal !

Great temple of Religion, and her twin sister dear,

Loved, cherished Liberty, whom freemen all revere—

Grand Temple reared by God, the Jews' and Gentiles' home,

The mountain-peaks thy spires, the concave sky thy dome ;

The lakes baptismal fonts, the cliffs thy altars which

Are filled with offerings sweet piled in profusion rich

High up unto the sky, fired by the lightning's flash—

As when the prophets false of Baal to abash,

In olden times, God sent fire down from Heaven and burned

Elijah's bullock fat, that thus it might be learned

Who was his minister, and who impostor vile,—

For this an angry frown, for that a gracious smile.

Grand Temple reared by God, the Jews' and Gentiles' home,

The mountain-peaks thy spires, the concave sky thy dome ;

Birds sing their songs of praise, old Ocean murmurs low,

Whose solemn organ-notes in streams of music flow—

Thy congregation great, millions of freemen true,

Who throng thy sacred aisles, and fill each open pew.

Columbia ! loved Columbia ! thou art a nation's pride ;

In grandeur, glory, strength all lands thou hast defied.

7

No equals, rivals few, e'er mayst thou hold such place,
Great God's own glorious work, thou land of noblest race!
Thrones totter to their base, and kingdoms falling crash,
As mad contention's waves around them fiercely dash;
Beneath war's mighty earthquake the Old World's empires reel,
Like vessels in a storm, when skies there wrath reveal.
But though commotions rage, Oh, thou my noble land,
As granite isle of sea as firm shall ever stand,
Around whose solid base, the foaming waves e'er dash,—
Against whose rock-ribbed sides the angry billows lash!

But are there some among old Europe's ruling mass,
Who say our honest boast, is but as " sounding brass ; "
And vow with earnestness, that young Columbia fair,
Her wreath of glory, pride, will not forever wear?
And do they challenge us to tell them why, when all
The ancient lands have fallen, our own shall never fall?

And are there some 'mong those who much do tyrants hate,
And our free land respect, who when they contemplate,

Of ancient, mighty lands, the grandeur and the power,

Some living centuries long, and others but an hour,

Still falling *all* at last, and lying in the dirt,

Unable to throw off Death's bonds which them begirt,—

Who lose their confidence that young Columbia fair

Oür wreath of glory, pride, as now, will ever wear,

And ask a reason for the hope which in *us* lies,

As bright as any star that gilds the azure skies?

We shall when we have oped the volume of the Past,

And seen how once arose and fell these kingdoms vast,

THE WORLD'S FIFTH EMPIRE.

CANTO FIFTH.

> But hold! — these dark, these perishing arcades,
> These mouldering plinths, these sad and blackened shafts,
> These vague entablatures, this broken frieze,
> These shattered cornices, this wreck, this ruin,
> These stones — alas! these gray stones, are they all,
> All of the proud and the colossal left
> By the corrosive hours to fate and me?
>
> EDGAR A. POE.

> Though every other land should fall, lie with the dead,
> While earth lasts, thou, *my land*, shalt rear thy noble head.
>
> ANONYMOUS.

See Roman Scipio great amid giant ruins stand,

While naught the silence breaks save heart-beats slow and grand!

He meditates alone and stirs his inmost soul;—

A mighty race he's run, and now has reached the goal;

And prostrate at his feet a fallen empire lies;—

She begs him not for peace, for death has closed her eyes.

Enwrapt in vision's mantle his statue there he stands!

The panorama long of ages clasping hands

Moves slowly on before with ever-varying scene;

Now dark with gloomy cloud, now bright with golden sheen.

And mighty structures wondrous here rise up toward the sky;

Oh! can such empires fall? and can such glory die?

The master minds of world have their foundations laid

In earth's firm centre, deep, and their proportions weighed.

But see, they totter now, while their tall columns crumble,

And 'neath the earthquake's shock, to earth from Heaven they

    tumble!

Then onward moves the canvass, and other empires shows,

Expanded germs of mind, as oak from acorn grows.

They have their rise, their strength, their dotage, and their fall;

Not all great glory reach, but death the doom of all!

Here rises "sacred Troy," with palaces and walls;

But soon the Grecians come;—she conquers or she falls.

Before her gates the host, with proud "Jove nourished kings;"

His armor Hector takes and out his Trojans brings.

Alas! cursed with the knowledge of what will be her doom,

He sees old Ilium strong soon wrapt in death-like gloom!

"I know the day will come when our great Troy shall fall—

Ah! Troy with her people, her glory and her all!"

Yes, e'en old Ilium fell, for destined not to stand,

She for her race become a mausoleum grand!

A remnant of her sons in fortune's hands are thrown;

Through perils great they pass, then reach a shore unknown.

And now on Terra's breast an infant in strength gains,—

Rome rises to the view, and o'er the world soon reigns.

Across the narrow sea, a rival rears her head;

The Romans she defies, though earth shake 'neath their tread.

And thrice in bloody combat, in wrath they grapple long;

Carthage at last grows weak, but old Rome in power strong.—

In ruins now Carthage lies, her walls fall to the ground,

And loud the victors' shouts through skies above resound.

The canvass now's unwound from the mighty wheel of Time,

And Scipio has viewed these awful scenes sublime!

He wakes him from his dream, and when he sees the fate
Of Rome's once giant rival, an empire once so great,
Then from the fountains deep of a great and noble heart,
Flow tears clear as the streams which from the mountains start ;
And quick across his mind, a strange thought flashes now,
And clouds in sorrow deep that sunlit, laureled brow,—
That such will be the fate of proud and mighty Rome,
The mistress of the world, his own, beloved home.
The words of Hector brave, he to himself repeats,
As moved he gazes on those sad, deserted streets :
" I know the day will come, when our great Troy shall fall—
Ah ! Troy with her whole race, her glory and her all !
And oh ! the day will come when Rome so great shall fall—
Old Rome with *her* whole race *her* glory and *her* all !"
Though in this vision grand, the panorama long
Showed some empires which stood and fell like giants strong,
Antiquity's thick mist, and the settling dust of ages,
Hid of time's strange history quite many and bright pages;
And as that canvass long there onward, onward rolled,
Oh ! many views there were which he could not behold.

But still he sees enough to make him ponder, and

Confess Rome too will fall, struck down by Death's fell hand.

But mystery queer and strange, oh ! why is it that he

Makes such prediction *now ?*—affirms the day will be,

When Rome with all her power shall pass away and die,

And in obscurity entombed there ever lie ?

Why such prediction *now,* when flushed with all the pride

Of a great conqueror, who stands there by the side

Of Rome's dead enemy—that Amazon whose strength

Had made her ever fear, till pierced, stretched out at length ?

It had not been so strange, if many years before,

When Hannibal the Great such fame and glory bore,—

When he marched to the Alps, and made those Titans bold

To doff their snowy plumes, and suppliant knee to hold,—

Yes, made those giants tall lie level with the ground,

(As his imperial trump the stern command did sound)

Acknowledging his might invincible and strong,

As o'er their prostrate forms he led his troops along,

And then swept down upon Italia's blooming plain

Like a mad avalanche where Death and Terror reign,—

If then some Roman had predicted she would fall,

And meet a fate but common or soon or late to all.—

It had not been so strange, if when a conquering foe

Had brought upon her fear and consternation, woe,—

Had scattered to the winds, like chaff before the mill,

Her legions brave and strong,—had baffled the courage, skill

Of every consul who with army had been sent

To stop his wild career, to heal the dangerous rent,

Which in Italia's side the cold and cruel blade,

Deep driven by victor's hand, had in his fury made,

Whence flowed in purple stream her life-blood dear and true,

As there drooped in agony her mild, soft eye of blue;

And fled the genial smile from her bright, sunny face;

And faded in her hair the flowers which once did grace;—

It had not been so strange, if when drear, black Despair

Had oped her sable wings, and dropped their shadow there

On every trembling heart; when Rumor flying fast,

Announced in quivering tones that hope for Rome was past,—

That thundering at her gates soon Hannibal would stand,

And soon her people die, and fall her temples grand;—

8

If at this dreadful hour when clouds hung like palls dark,

And when her star of hope had ceased to cast a spark,—

If then some Roman had predicted she would fall,

And meet a fate but common or soon or late to all;—

It had not been so strange, e'en if he had then said,

That through the future's veil he saw Rome with the dead.

But for one thus to speak, when after even more

Than one whole century, with short intervals, the door—

A flood-gate through which long had flowed war's purple tide—

Of Janus' temple grand, that had stood open wide,

Thus indicating that Bellona fierce and Mars

Rode raging through the air in their swift, blood-washed cars,

Attended by Discord, and Clamor, and Anger, Fear,

Who with them e'er were wont 'midst war's din to appear,

And make the world resound with their loud shout and cry,

As they in hurry mad flew 'tween the earth and sky;—

But for one thus to speak, when after even more

Than one whole century, with short intervals, the door,

Which had thus open stood, was closed to tell mankind

Peace had resumed the seat old War had now resigned;—

When after struggling hard one hundred years and more,

With pauses that they might their energies restore ;—

When after wrestling long old Carthage had gone down,

Ne'er more to make Rome fear her menace or her frown,—

Now thus for him to speak is very strange indeed,

Triumphant, seeing all his cherished plans succeed ;

Knowing that Rome is now the mistress of the world,

When her last rival has thus from her throne been hurled.

Because all other lands of ages gone and past,

After a life-time short, grew weak and fell at last,

As natural consequence, must she meet this sad doom,

And lie down too, as they, in gloomy ruin's tomb?

Has she no principle immortal, great and strong,—

Does no peculiar virtue unto old Rome belong,

Which will make her o'er the entire world to reign,

With all its conquered princes there marching in her train,

Till old Destruction fierce shall throw his arms at length

Around earth's pillars tall, and then with all his strength

The structure great bring down, with loud, terrific sound,

In universal ruin thus all things to confound!

"But, Scipio, oh! why is·it that thou dost lose

All of thy confidence—while standing there to muse—

In the eternity of old Rome's giant life,

Now wholly freed by thee from fear and war and strife?

Thou art a patriot true, thou lovest thy great land,

And though earth's mistress now, thou say'st she cannot stand!"

Thus speaks Rome's anxious, good, protecting deity,

And asks cause for his doubts of her the great and free.

He answers not a word, but doth his statue stand;

The silence naught breaks save his heart-beats slow and grand!

For Fate invisible, as past him she doth fly,

Low mutters in his ear with sad and doleful cry:

"Ah! yes, the day will come, when Rome so great shall fall,

Old Rome with *her* whole race, *her* glory, and *her* all!"

But oh! my countrymen, is there among you one,

Who living day by day 'neath Liberty's bright sun,

Upon that spot could stand, where Alexander great

Once stood, and gazed, and thought upon sad Troy's fate,

While owls in mockery droll hooted from crumbling wall,

And rank and poisonous vines embraced the columns tall,

Which here and there yet stood to mark old Ilium's site,

Past glory's monuments and fame's, once grand and bright;—

Oh! say, could one of you standing on that lone shore,

Where that great man once stood and read his Homer o'er;—

Read how his ancestors had laid her in the dust,

Assisted by the gods in a cause righteous, just—

Then, there dare to repeat old Hector's words of fame,

And then and there predict Columbia's fate the same?

Go to Thermopylæ, and stand there where once stood

Leonidas with his three hundred Spartans good,

And there for many days, in that bold mountain-pass,

Invincible withstood the great invading mass

Of Persian armies vast, like rugged cliffs which stand

As gray, grim giants tall, and e'er protect the land,

By beating back the waves of sea with rage convulsed,

Which might o'erwhelm the earth unless by these repulsed;—

Go sit where once there sat, upon his throne of gold,

Xerxes the Great, and watched — as from his aerie bold,

The warlike eagle doth, with joy, expected prey —

For a great victory, soon, and honors of the day;—

Sit there and read how Greece was saved by Grecian men,

How scores of Persian ships were sunk or taken then ;—

Then visit Marathon that glorious battle field,

On which two hundred thousand Persians once did yield

Their lives to Erebus, by Grecia's warriors sent

To deep Tartarean shades there ever to be pent,—

That battle field on which they to old Persia taught

That all her driven slaves and gold and show could naught

Avail against a land, where freemen thought and felt,

Where to the despot's rod, no valiant soul e'er knelt—

And then read how Greece fell, old Greece called in her day

The cradle of science, arts, where learning first held sway,—

How she who conquered Troy, and then the world entire,

By Rome at last was hurled into the dust and mire,—

And then and there repeat old Hector's words of fame,

And, if you can, predict Columbia's fate the same!

And oh! my countrymen, is there among you one

Who living day by day 'neath Liberty's bright sun,

Upon that spot could stand where Scipio the Great

Once stood, and thought and gazed on Carthage and her fate ;—

Oh! say, could one of you, now standing on the place
Where once sat Afric's queen, that queen of power and grace,
There buried far beneath the heaped up sands of Time,
With scarce a stone to mark her name once so sublime;—
Oh! say, could one of you, whilst pondering deeply there,
Let fall those words of Hector upon the silent air,
And then like Scipio reasoning declare and feel her doom
An emblem of the fate, your land will wrap in gloom!

And now, Columbia's sons, read old Rome's famous story,
With all its many leaves so gilt with gold and glory,—
Read how "Æneas pious" led his small band so brave,
Through tortuous pilgrimage across the ocean wave,
Deserting their loved homes now held by conquering foe;
And choosing thus to wander, and suffering every woe;
Preferring toils and trials to slavery's heavy chains,
Well known to be the fate of each one that remains
Among all Troy's ruins, which cover all the ground,
While through her bloody streets the Grecians steps resound;—
How after trials, afflictions, and perils, troubles far
Too many here to name, the bright and golden star

Of Hope arose, and shone high o'er Italia's shore,

Causing their hearts to throb with joy ne'er known before;—

How after many years an empire raised her head,

And shook at last the earth, 'neath her firm, giant tread;

And how her conquering eagle flew fast from land to land,

Subjecting nations all to his supreme command;

E'en Greece escaping not, Greece great and glorious, old,

The mother of warriors strong, e'en Alexander bold,

Who from the chaos dark first lifted many a stone,

And built an edifice, like earth scarce e'er has known,

And then sat down and wept—this architect so great—

Because through all the world he found no other state

To break to pieces, whence, materials to supply

To raise his structure grand still higher toward the sky,

That he might so ascend up to the heavens, and,

There deified, be worshiped, a god august and grand;—

Then read how Rome, the queen, who o'er the earth once

      reigned,—

How Rome, whose honored name had such great glory gained,

Who conquered mighty Greece and Carthage and others too,

The greatest empire which the ancients ever knew,

At last was overwhelmed by fierce barbarians wild,

Such men as she had oft in heaps of thousands piled

On many a battle field, while cold and dead they stared,

As offerings to her gods, their wrath thus to be spared,—

Such men as she had oft tied to her chariot great,

As in her triumphs proud she rode in pompous state.—

Go visit *every* land beneath God's glorious sun,

Where still some ruin stands to tell what once was done,

Pointing with finger lank of hard and chilling stone

To pages in history past, for tale of fame once known

Throughout the whole, wide world, though scarcely heard of now,

So blindly do mankind unto the Present bow;—

Go read the stories all of earth's chief empires great,

Whose heroes famous were in arts and war, and state;—

Yes, see and read all this, my countrymen, oh! yes,

And falter, if you can, in belief which we express,

That our Columbia fair, in all her pride shall be,

As long as God lets stand the earth and rolling sea;—

Yes, e'en then, if you can, utter these mournful lines,

As in your gloomy sky the star of Hope declines:—

"I know the day will come, when our great Troy shall fall,
Ah! Troy with her whole race, her glory, and her all!
And oh! I know that our Columbia great shall fall,
Columbia with *her* race, *her* glory, and *her* all!"

But it was promised we would tell the sceptic why
We had such confidence Columbia ne'er would die.
Perhaps, should one see this he'd laugh in very glee,
And say what we have said but strengthens doubts which he
Had always thus possessed, by bringing to his mind,
Afresh the olden tales which we in history find;
And vow it would not take a prophet great to tell
That our land too would go, for others older fell.
Have patience, sir, and we will now soon tell you why
We have such confidence Columbia ne'er will die.
We will a difference show in the character and stamp
Of civilization which marked those whose mighty tramp
May still be faintly heard, e'en to this distant day,
Along the corridors of ages past away!

THE WORLD'S FIFTH EMPIRE.

CANTO SIXTH.

Westward the course of empire takes its way.
The first four acts already past,
The fifth shall close the drama with the day —
Time's noblest empire is its last.

BISHOP BERKLEY.

And the rain descended, and the floods came, and the winds blew and beat upon
that house; and it fell not: for it was founded upon a rock.

MATT. vii. 25.

The volume of the Past, since first we oped and read,

Has told us much indeed, how by the giant tread

Of mad Destruction strong, or Progress great, the world

Was shaken, as in turn his banner each unfurled.

But for a long time we have scanned but those worn pages

Which treat of only ancient, and dim, beclouded ages;

So nearer to our times it now behooves to turn,

And from this ponderous book still reading, try to learn

What thus we may by glance, and then proceed to show
Why we may think our land — the greatest earth doth know
Shall last as long as this great globe whereon we live,
Which rounded by his hand God once did motion give.

Now many hundred years on fleeting wing have flown,
Since those of which we read as empires great were known.
The middle ages now have come, and all the sky
Is hung in mourning robes of clouds of blackest dye.
O'er all the world's broad map our weary eyes we throw;
But on no land the star of Progress seems to glow.
To gross licentiousness, effeminacy, weak,
Old Asia's given up, and Truth dares not to speak.
Here e'en Jerusalem, where Christ once lived and taught,
By infidels' strong chains to bondage hard is brought.
And poor black Africa is hid, enveloped in
Dark superstition's night, idolatry and sin.
Europe—she loudly groans under a leaden weight,
Prostrated to the earth, big with transgression's fate.
No land we find where pure Religion is revered;
Where Liberty's fair robes with blood are never smeared;

Where Peace her snowy flag unfurls and holds command,
And Truth's white breast is pierced by dart from no fell hand.

But lo!—on yonder mount methinks I see a light
Spreading its rays afar, illumining the night.
A flaming banner floats 'mid darkness most profound,
Dispelling fast the clouds like vultures hanging 'round.
And now a giant form majestic rises there ;
A mighty trump then sounds upon the trembling air,
Whose notes like thunder-peals among the crags resound;
And like an earthquake shakes with fear the very ground.
And then these words are heard far rolling loud and clear.
" Hark, all ye men of earth, I bid ye me to hear ;
The HERALD OF DESTINY, I through the future see :—
Be still, keep silence now, and list ye well to me."

The Book of Fate he oped, this short exordium passed,
And as he spake his words rang like the bugle's blast:
" Now four successive empires the universal world
Have ruled, and each by other from power such was hurled!

The Babylonian first, and next the Persian vast;

And then the Grecian grand, next Rome, not least though last.

Great Babylon first falls, next Persia's with the dead;

No more now trembles earth 'neath Grecian phalanx' tread—

And proud old Rome then falls — the City of Seven Hills —

Each struggles long with Death, but dies, for God thus wills!

"The Future's curtains dark I now shall draw aside,

And give you but a glimpse, as time will onward glide.

The drama's not complete — but *four* acts have been played,

The fifth is yet to come, though for sometime delayed.

'Tis true that kingdoms many, yes kingdoms great and small,

Before this act comes on shall rise, but soon they'll fall.

No universal empire the world shall ever see,

Until established firm this last one great shall be.

"Now in the northern ocean an island rears her head,

And Albion is her name, a name to love and dread.

But though this mighty queen a sceptre great shall wield,

The earth to her shall never supreme dominion yield.

But then this ocean queen a daughter is to bear, —

A scion of noble stock, a creature good and fair;

And then the star of Progress shall westward take its way,

And this young daughter follow its mild and golden ray.

And in a new world vast across the rolling sea,

An empire she shall found; the fifth one this will be.

And based upon Religion — that firm, abiding rock —

It shall all tempests scorn, nor fear the earthquake's shock.

And as I now proclaim, let all the earth take heed,

The last shall be the greatest, — for God has thus decreed!"

Conscious his words will roll e'er 'mong the hills of time

He ceases now to speak — one moment stands sublime!

A cloud rests on his brow all gilt with golden light,

Forming an awful crown, so strange, half dark, half bright;

Then disappears from view, as Night her curtains black

Around the towering mount unfolds and now drops back.

But like the circling waves, when Sinbad's eagle threw

In the sea his rock of tons, as mad above he flew,

Which onward, onward rushed, until they beat the land;

Thus rolled his words along like thunder wild and grand,

Till, moving fast, they strike Eternity's far shore,

And echoed back from thence, resound the world all o'er!

"And based upon Religion—that firm, abiding rock—

It shall all tempests scorn, nor fear the earthquake's shock."

And now let those among old Europe's down-trod mass,

Who say our honest boast is but as sounding brass,

And vow with earnestness that young Columbia fair

Her wreath of glory, pride, will not forever wear;—

And let those too 'mong them, who though they tyrants hate,

And our free land respect;—who (when they contemplate

Of ancient, mighty lands the grandeur and the power,

Some living centuries long and others but an hour,

Still falling all at last, and lying in the dirt,

Unable to throw off Death's bonds which them begirt)

Then waver in their belief that our Republic great

Can stand forever when to die seems other's fate;—

And if among *us*, too, there be a timid few,

Who casting back their eyes for retrospective view

Along the vista dim of ages past away,

And seeing mighty ruins there standing grim and gray,

Amid mysterious gloom, like spectral giants tall,

More awful, fearful still while robed in darkness' pall;

Those who, like Scipio great moved by his trance and dream,

In strength of their own land their faith to lose would seem,

Of sanguine nature not, revolving in the mind

The doom which all those lands inevitably find;

And seeing strength depart much faster than it e'er

Was known to come to one, experience sometimes fear

For the eternity of their own country good,

Thinking she may not stem the tide which none withstood—

Who, if they had firm faith (with which poor Peter might

Have walked the troubled seas, and felt not doubt or fright)

Could move along serene, and hopeful faces wear,

Instead of sinking down in absolute despair,

Without that helping staff, when mad waves agitate

The waters o'er which sail our glorious ship of State!—

Let all who doubt or fear, where'er their lot is thrown,

Hear what to freemen bold, has long been felt and known,

"And based upon religion—that firm, abiding rock—

It shall all tempests scorn, nor fear the earthquake's shock!"

That rock rejected by all other builders, thus

Becomes the corner's head—a base used but by us.

Oh! yes, my countrymen, thus can ye boldly say,

Columbia ne'er will fall—not till the Final Day.

Here's reason for the hope, which e'er within you lies,

As bright as brightest star, which gilds the azure skies!

A great, inherent virtue, firm principle and strength

Makes her exempt from death—all other's fate at length—

Till God shall earth destroy, and hurl its structures down,

Low crouching in their fall before his awful frown!

Though Carthage, Rome, and Greece have fallen, she shall stand.

Here differs she from them—our great, beloved land.

Those who their bases laid and reared them toward the sky

Did not them consecrate to Lord of all on high;

But in *her* corner-stone the Bible true was placed,

And as the building rose its walls with texts were graced,

And prayers were offered up that this might ever be

A refuge for the poor—a temple Lord to Thee!

Without foundation such no land can long here stand;

'Twere like unto a house built not on rock but sand,

Which, when the streams beat hard, would fall and float away

Adown the tide which runs to Desolation's bay.

And more especially no great Republic, where

All men, as it would seem, authority must bear,—

Where each one governs some, and walks as if a king,

And Justice tardy may quick judgment not e'er bring;

As in a government where one strong, single will

Rules absolute, and has the power to save or kill.

No, here there should exist the power of self-restraint

Within the breast of each, that passion's moral taint,

Or overwhelming tide, might fail to have effect;

That gross injustice, wrong, should stern rebuke expect,

Arraigned before the great tribunal secret, bold,

Of conscience, that strong bar more dread than that of old

Venice, the " Ocean Queen,"—the "Council of the Ten,"

Whose trials and punishments 'tis useless here to pen,

Wrapped as is too well known in gloom and darkness dread,

Awful as that which veils the chambers of the dead!—

Yes, power of self-restraint, offspring of Conscience, which
Is lit with light of Truth, divine, and bright, and rich.

Two thousand years ago old, hoary monarch Time
A great Republic built in Grecia's golden clime,
Upon whose massive walls were by degrees inscribed
Morality's pure tenets, which thus her sons imbibed;
And Wisdom's teachings good, and Virtue's doctrines true,
And sound Philosophy's great principles they knew;
But founded not upon that rock we named before,
When fierce commotion's waves its base unstable tore,
This structure, though it reared its lofty head above
The very clouds, fell down, and great the fall thereof.

And not long afterwards a great Republic strong,
Built to defy the world, was thrown to earth headlong,
By billows wild and mad of cruel civil wars,
Although its head sublime once struck the very stars!
Rome, founded not upon this rock, now lay her down
In dark oblivion's grave, beneath Destruction's frown!

And sixty years ago, after a flow of blood

Had swept o'er France, a strong, and fierce, and raging flood,

And borne down in its tide all order, law, and rule,

And whirled the wild debris in ruin's gloomy pool;

And all the temples grand of Justice and God too

Had undermined and crushed as on its billows flew,—

As if then coming down from Heaven's high golden gate,

To punish Gallia's sons, an avenging angel great

Had stretched his mighty wand o'er all this wicked land,

And then had sent on her, by God's most just command,

A curse like that which once upon poor Egypt fell,

When Aaron, all her sons' rebellious hearts to quell,

Raised up his arm and smote the waters with his rod,

And everywhere it seemed blood's demons there had trod!—

Yes sixty years ago after all this had been,

A government arose conceived in wrong and sin;

Republican 'twas called, built on "*fraternal right.*"

The Bible thrown aside, then all was wrapped in night!.

Based on the shifting sand it fell with mighty crash,

And in its fall became a mass of ruins, trash!

And two long centuries have passed since o'er the sea,

Our Pilgrim Fathers came, the tyrant's rod to flee.

And in the New World vast they then commenced to build

A monument whose fame the whole wide earth has filled,—

A noble monument to God and Liberty,

Constructed by the hands of patriots great and free.

Yes, on old Plymouth Rock they there began to rear—

With that for solid base—their structure grand and dear;

And still the glorious work as yet goes bravely on,

Although two hundred years have now elapsed and gone,

As Time's great chariot-wheels revolved on axle hot,

His strong steeds moving e'er in long and measured trot.

Each state is but a stone in this vast edifice;—

Oh! what can all earth show which can compare with this?

Yes, year by year, a block is added there, but still

A century may pass before each space they fill.

And when each stone is laid, when e'en all this is done,

This mighty glorious work will be but just begun.

The principles and rules of science and of art,

And maxims for the mind, and truths for mankind's heart;

Religion's doctrines great, and all real literature;

All in philosophy or virtue good and pure;

All that is known in state and politics, and laws, —

In fact all that concerns humanity's great cause,

Must on its massive walls be deep inscribed by hand

Of Justice and of Truth, — we think it God's command!

That much of this e'en now has been completed, true;

But long as earth shall last much there will be to do.

Hail! Monument to God and Liberty most dear;

Temple of Knowledge rich, as firm as now stand e'er!

Oh! yes, all hail to thee, great Learning's institute!

Before thy sculptured walls old Error stands there mute.

Grand University for our whole human race!

Where all may come and learn their minds and hearts to grace,

Great oceans lave thy base, as firm as earth's and deep; —

Thy head is bathed in clouds as fleeting past they sweep!

Was such an edifice e'er seen, though not yet done?

Did such a one e'er stand beneath God's glorious sun?

And still must we now say that there are some who live

In its broad shadows cool, whose hearts no thanks would give,

No gratitude would show, for benefits received?

And do we speak the truth, and will it be believed

That there are some in each extensive, prosperous state,

Who like mean traitors act, and like poor madmen prate;

And on the freeman's name cast thus black, foul disgrace,

And try to pull "*their*" block—Shame, blush and hide thy face-

From this grand structure high, unconscious when one stone

Is taken from its walls, the whole to earth is thrown,

A mass of ruins great whose loud terrific shock

Will crush our race and make the universe to rock!

Oh! God, we trust in thee in each convulsion small

Or great; in mighty storm, or in the blustering squall.

Give us e'er pilots true to guide the ship of State

Among the treacherous rocks, and through each dangerous strai

Oh! give us e'er the men who may be equal to

All great emergencies;—who will their duty do —

A Washington, a Scott, a Webster, or a Clay,

As circumstances need a man to lead the way.

Now when contentions fierce political would shake

The glorious fabric of our commonwealth and make

The hopeful tremble e'en, now, oh! God, give us one,

Like old Kentucky's great and patriotic son,

Who, when mad waves durst dash in fury and in rage

Against his country's bark, their wrath could e'er assuage,

As lifting up his hand commanding, he would say,

"Hark! billows, peace, be still!" while they would him obey,

And passive sink to rest, acknowledging the power

Of him who them could curb, while standing firm as tower

Which, on some rocky coast, the winds and waves repel,

Whene'er 'gainst Neptune's rule they rising up rebel.

Yes, "founded on Religion—that firm, abiding rock—

She shall all tempests scorn, nor fear the earthquake's shock."

Yes, 'neath Jehovah's eye thus she shall stand fore'er

Unless we recreant prove to our own interests dear,

As ancient Israel did, whose country, firmly based

Upon God's written Law, all dangers boldly faced,

Till too rebellious much his chosen race became,

And for their wickedness their land met fate the same

As other countries, and, as prophecy had said,

Her walls fell down before the Romans' mighty tread,

10

So that on other lay not e'en one single stone,

And ploughed up were the sites from which they had been thrown!

Columbia! loved Columbia! thou art a nation's pride;

In grandeur, glory, fame, all lands thou hast defied;—

No equals, rivals few, e'er mayst thou hold such place,

Great God's own glorious work, thou land of noblest race!

Though true that we are proud, and love to boast of thee,

The honor we give Him who made thee such to be.

A great king's mournful fate stands like a monument,

Reminding us to whom we owe the glory lent.

"Is not this Babylon, which was built strong by me,

By my own might and power, and for my majesty!"

Exclaimed a monarch grand, as full of pride he walked,

In his great palace fine, and to himself thus talked,

While contemplating all the noble structures reared

In strength and beauty as they to him thus appeared.

But while the word was still in his proud mouth, there fell

A voice from Heaven, saying, "Hark, man, to what I tell.

Nebuchadnezzar, king, tis spoken thus to thee,

Thy kingdom is now lost, and from men shalt thou flee,

And make thy dwelling with the beasts that roam the field,

Where grass, which feeds the ox, food for thee too shall yield;

And seven times seven shall pass o'er thee till thou doth know

God rules empires and gives to whom he will bestow."

And true it is that in the same hour was the thing

Fulfilled upon this great, but proud and boastful king.

But oh! my countrymen, how grateful should we be,

That we have such a land, as this vast one we see.

Oh! great prerogative it is herein to live!

To Him all honor who doth life and being give.

Through endless ages yet our land shall still exist

If we in patriotism and virtue e'er persist.

With her would die the hopes of Earth's down-trodden mass,

Who turn their eyes to her amid their chains, alas!

And sigh for liberty, e'en as the prisoner sighs,

When looking through his bars, he views the beaming skies;

While kings and monarchs would then shout aloud for glee,

And 'round her funeral bier dance in wild revelry.

Thrones tremble while she lives, they shook e'en at her birth,

And well all princes know that ours would be on earth

The last example of self-government, and hence

They watch her rapid growth with jealousy intense,

Uneasy when they see the giantess grow fast;

Rejoicing when they see dissension's seeds broadcast.

Oh! then, my countrymen, let not discord and strife

Divide our glorious land, take Liberty's dear life.

Oh! whisper not "disunion," oh! utter not such cry—

It makes the patriot grieve, it makes the angel sigh!

A grander destiny awaits Columbia's pride,

For she is to extend her domain far and wide,

And by her great example to conquer all the world,

Until old Tyranny from every throne is hurled,

And Knowledge to and fro has run and been increased,

And Sin's and Error's rule upon our globe has ceased!

Years after years may pass and centuries roll away;

All other lands may fall, their glory fade from day;

Even the mother-country, the one who gave her birth,

But she shall ever stand, God's own firm throne on earth,

Till the Lion of Judah's tribe doth open the sixth seal,

And lo! an earthquake great its terrors wild reveal;

And the sun becomes as black as sackcloth of hair, e'en;

The moon a pool of blood losing its silver sheen;

And to the earth the stars from their sky headlong fall,

As fig-tree casts her figs, untimely in the squall;

And the heavens disappear as a scroll together rolled;

And mountains, islands all, are moved from place they hold;

And kings of earth, men great, the rich men, and the chief

Captains, and mighty men, and bond, and free, in reef

And den themselves there hide, and to the mountains say,

"Fall on us, hide us from the face of Him alway

Upon the golden throne; alas! conceal us from

The Lamb's avenging wrath, for his wrath's day has come!

Before his angry frown who able now to stand?"—

Then, not till then, shall fall our great and glorious land.

But till that day, e'en that, shall stand this mighty land,

Like giant mountain-cliff colossal, firm, and grand,

Around whose hoary head the vivid lightnings play,

Gilding his crown of clouds with fire of diamond ray;

While all the storms that beat his rock-ribbed sides, but make

More adamantine still, yet ever fail to shake—

While Ocean's phalanx waves are thrown in disarray,

And scattered to the winds, mere mists, are blown away

As flying swift along like cavalry in charge

In wrath the foam they cast from jaws distended, large,

And strive to batter down this bulwark of the land,

That they may overrun, like dragoons sword in hand—

While to the earthquake's great, invisible, strange power,

Which hurls down in its march man's strongest wall and tower,

The veteran nods his head, inclines his mighty form,—

But not because he fears the subterranean storm—

As monarch monarch gives in honor a compliment,

Respectful recognition;—thus is his body bent!

Until the Lord's day come, e'en as a thief in night,

And the heavens pass away with great noise and affright;

Until the elements shall melt with fervent heat,

And earth and works therein by fire their last end meet—

Yes, till that day, e'en that, shall stand this mighty land,

Like giant mountain-cliff colossal, firm, and grand!

MY MOTHER.

COLERIDGE.

My Mother dear,

I draw me near

To talk with you, and round your neck

To throw my arms, where oft I've hung

In infancy,—where tight I've clung

When little terrors frightened me;

As trembling vine will hug its tree,

When earth mad Giant Storm would wreck!

My Mother sweet,

As now you greet

My unexpected book you see,

Know that, perhaps, 'tis owed to you,

That these poetic flowers we view,

'Neath your approving smile so kind,

E'er grew from buds which filled my mind;—

The honor's yours — if honor be.

My Mother dear,

Think this not queer,

For I but give you credit due:

Cannot remember many a time,

When I'd bring you my childlike rhyme,

You me would help, encourage:—"Fine!

My Jamie, you are bound to shine!"—

And then would you correct it through.

My Mother mild,

When I, a child,

My little, boyish pranks would play,

But seldom would a darksome frown

Fall with its chilling shadow down

Upon my spirits' sparkling stream

Lit bright with young life's joyous gleam; —

You loved to see me free and gay.

My Mother firm, —

I justly term

You thus—quite resolute, not rash;

For true, by nature though you be

Most mild, with gentle heart and free,

Yet when stern Duty gives her call,

You stand as firm as granite wall,

'Gainst which in vain the billows dash.

My Mother learned,

With mind well turned

And studded thick with gems of thought,

Where poetry's flowers all gaily bloom,

And shed around their rich perfume,

You have an intellect deep, strong,—

Through which bright ideas trip along,—

And with true Learning's precepts fraught.

My Mother kind,

You are not blind

To poverty;—although descent

Through long and honored, noble race

Is traced;—though you have wealth and place,

You spurn not poor; for once, you tell,

Misfortune on *your* family fell,

And the golden bird flapped wings and went.

My Mother true,

I ne'er one knew

Who had herself more faithful shown

In all relations of this life,—

A truer or more faithful wife,—

Or mother, sister, Christian too;—

As all these you your duty do.

Truth has in your true heart a throne.

My Mother good,

Oh! that there would

Be more such Christians, as you here,

In this cold, strange, and troubled world,

In which life's bark is often whirled,

As a ship in Norway's maelstrom wild;—

But Christ your pilot, faithful child

Of his, oh! nothing do you fear.

My Mother gay,

Although the day

Of your bright youth has long passed by,

The gayest of the gay I trow

You are when joy sits on the brow,

And Wit from his electric hand

Through willing minds of social band

Sends meteoric sparks to fly.

My Mother old,—

But this I hold

In years, not in your feelings, no,—

Time's cunning hand yet fails to rob

The warm and sympathetic throb

From your kind heart—no heart of steel,

It for the bright and young can feel;—

Oh! may it never older grow!

My Mother dear,

I draw me near

To talk with you, and round your neck

To throw my arms, where oft I've hung

In infancy,—where tight I've clung

When little terrors frightened me;

As trembling vine will hug its tree,

When earth mad Giant Storm would wreck!

THE HARP OF A THOUSAND STRINGS.

If in this world of ours there be a harp
Strung with a thousand strings, the human heart
Must be that harp, from whose mysterious chords,
When struck by hand of a skillful player, roll
Those notes so varied and innumerable,
Which whisper of the hopes and fears, the woes
And joys, that ofttimes swell within the soul
Of mortal man.
       Down in old Ocean's caves
Glow pearls, which none but artful diver e'er
May bring to light of day; and from the deep

Depths of the organ grand, which stands beneath

The gothic arch of some cathedral old—

A monument of ages past—may he,

Whose soul 's been bathed in music's fount by his

Own muse, bring forth those sparkling gems of sound,

Those solemn tones and sweet, melodious notes,

Which, rise majestic up to Heaven's bright gates.

And twining round the silver chords with which

The human heart is strung, as growing vines

Cling to their slender twigs, is melody,

Such as none ever may bring forth save the great

MUSICIAN OF THE SOUL, the Poet, who

Although upon the earth, doth yet from his

High stand-point there look down, *external* from the world—

The Poet who can soothe, caress, excite,

Inspire, as with the magic, skillful touch

His practiced hand steals gently o'er, or flies,

Like lightning's flash through high sky's azure vault,

Along this deep and thousand-chorded, heaven-strung

Instrument; and thus produces feelings,

Emotions, corresponding with his own;

E'en till in unison, sweet harmony

So beautiful, its every string strikes with

His breathing harp's each chord,—such sympathy!—

The Poet, the heart's interpreter; yes, he

Whose piercing, eagle eye may penetrate

Into the central depths of heart within

A heart, and read and teach to other souls

Those thoughts, those passions deep, which many oft

May feel and know, but few can e'er express.—

The Poet who from nature looketh up

To nature's God; yes, gazeth from the earth

To Heaven, speaking for strange mortality

To its Creator the "thoughts that breathe and words

That burn," in language such as angels use.

TO MY NIECE.

LINES ADDRESSED TO MY NIECE,

M. B. B.

UPON HER SEVENTEENTH BIRTHDAY.

O, Mary dear!
Another year
Has come, has waned, has passed;
And "sweet sixteen,"
That garland green,
Has faded now at last!

Thy childhood soon—
That happy boon—
Will womanhood assume,
As half-blown rose
Soon bursts and grows
Into perfection's bloom!

11

But though a child
So bright and wild,
Not long thou still wilt be;
Yet ever may
Thy spirits gay
Be light as now and free!

'Tis true thy heart,
Affliction's dart
Has oft pierced through and through;
Yet still that sting
Time's soothing wing
Has fanned and healed anew.

'Tis true thy head,
Before Death's tread,
In grief and sorrow deep,
Has bowed as flower
On Nature's bower
Before the storm's wild sweep! —

Yet like that flower,
By God's own power
Thy face again did rise
To smile, and thus
To gladden us,—
To cheer us with bright eyes.

We love thy smile
So void of guile;
Thy heart sincere and free;—
The same gay child,
So bright and wild,
Oh! couldst thou ever be!

A gushing stream
With sparkling gleam
All through thy heart there flows;
And on its shore
With head drooped o'er
A smiling blossom grows,

What flower is this,
Which oft doth kiss
Those waters wild and free?
That flower is love,
Brought from above,—
That love is love for me!

A gushing stream
With sparkling gleam
All through *my* heart there flows;
And on its shore
With head drooped o'er
A smiling blossom grows.

What flower is this,
Which oft doth kiss
Those waters wild and free?
That flower is love,
Brought from above,—
That love is love for *thee!*

Those rich, dear flowers
From Heaven's own bowers
Some angel bright placed there.
Oh! may their bloom
And sweet perfume
Our hearts forever bear!

DAR-THULA.*

"It may not be improper here to give the story which is the foundation of
this poem, as it is handed down by tradition. Usnoth, lord of Etha, which is
probably that part of Argyleshire which is near Loch Eta, an arm of the sea
in Lorn, had three sons, Nathos, Althos, and Ardan, by Slissáma, the daughter of Semo, and sister to the celebrated Cathullin. The three brothers,
when very young, were sent over to Ireland by their father, to learn the use
of arms under their uncle Cathullin, who made a great figure in that kingdom. They were just landed in Ulster when the news of Cathullin's death
arrived. Nathos though very young, took the command of Cathullin's army,
made head against Cairbar the usurper, and defeated him in several battles.
Cairbar at last, having found means to murder Cormac, the lawful king,
the army of Nathos shifted sides, and he himself was obliged to return into
Ulster, in order to pass over into Scotland.

Dar-thula, the daughter of Colla, with whom Cairbar was in love, resided
at that time in Seláma, a castle in Ulster. She saw, fell in love, and fled with
Nathos; but a storm rising at sea, they were unfortunately driven back on
that part of the coast of Ulster where Cairbar was encamped with his army.

The three brothers, after having defended themselves for some time with
great bravery, were at last overpowered and slain, and the unfortunate Dar-
thula killed herself upon the body of her beloved Nathos.

The poem opens on the night preceding the death of the sons of Usnoth,
and brings in, by way of episode, what passed before. It relates the death of
Dar-thula differently from the common tradition. This account is the most
probable, as suicide seems to have been unknown in those early times, no
traces of it being found in the old poetry."

* See Preface.

"The harp in Selma was not idly strung;
And long shall last the themes our poet sung."

O moon! daughter of high heaven, fair art thou!
Pleasant the silence of thy face, as now
In all thy loveliness thou dost step out,
The stars attending thy smooth, azure route.
Rejoice all the clouds in thy presence bright,
Their dark-brown sides glowing beneath thy light.
Lamp of still night, who like thee in the sky?
Before thy face the stars ashamed are shy,
And turn away their sparkling eyes.

      But say,
Whither dost thou retire from thy course alway,
When darksome then thy countenance doth grow?
Hath thou a hall, like Ossian, where thou mayest go?
Dwellest thou in the shadow of grief's black frown?
Have thy sisters fallen from high Heaven down?

Are they, who once rejoiced with thee no more?

Ah! yes, fair light, and thou dost mourn them sore.

But thou one night shalt leave thy blue path too;

And then the stars will lift their heads anew;

And they who were ashamed again feel joy;

But thou hast brightness now without alloy.

Burst the clouds, O wind, that this daughter fair

Of night may now look forth from her course there,

And all the shaggy mountains thus grow bright;

And ocean roll its snowy waves in light!

Nathos and Althos, beams of youth, now steer

The deep; and Ardan is his brothers near.

But then what form is that dim by their side,

Whose beauty thus the darksome night doth hide?

On ocean's growing wind her soft hair sighs;

While her long robe in dusky wreaths light flies.

She's like Heaven's spirit fair 'mid shadowy mist!

Save Dar-thula, Erin's first maid, who is 't?

From Cairbar's love with Nathos doth she flee.

The winds, Dar-thula, have deceived now thee;

They woody Etha to thy sails deny.
These are not thy loved hero's mountains high;
Nor is that sound his climbing waves' roar clear:
Cairbar's hills are nigh; their forms his towers rear;
Erin her head extends into the sea;
Tura's bay the ship receives.   Where have ye
Been, ye southern winds, deceiving thus her love?
Chasing the thistle's beard the plains above?
Oh! that ye had been rustling in this sail,
Till Etha's hills arose their chief to hail!
From home long absent, Nathos, hast been thou;
Alas! the day of thy return 's passed now!
But lovely to a strange land didst thou appear,
Lovely in the eyes of thy Dar-thula dear.
Thy face was like the morning's golden light;
Thy hair as black as raven's wing of night;
Thy soul like the hour of setting sun did seem;
Thy words were reeds' wind—Lora's gliding stream!
But when war rose thou wast a sea in storm!
The clang of thy arms was terrible; the swarm

12

Vanished away at sound of thy course bold.

Dar-thula did at such time thee behold,

As she on top of her mossy tower knelt—

Selàma's tower strong, where her fathers dwelt.

"O stranger!" cried she, "thou art lovely there,"

For her trembling soul arose, "thou art fair

In battle thou friend of fallen Cormac dead.

Why dost thou in thy wild valor rush ahead?

Why onward rush, youth of the ruddy cheek?

Against dark-brown Cairbar thy hands are weak!

Oh! that I might now from his love be free,

And in the presence of Nathos e'er happy be!

Blest Etha's rocks! his steps at the chase they'll know,

See his white breast, when winds his long hair blow."

Dar-thula, in Selàma's mossy tower

Thus didst thou speak—but round thee night doth lower;

The winds have now deceived thy sails, and high

Their roar.   O north wind, cease to whistle by,

Awhile, that I may hear that lovely one;—

Thy words are sweet when 'tween the blasts they run.

"Are these the rocks of Nathos?" then said she,
" This the roaring of his streams wild and free?
From Usnoth's nightly hall comes that light's bar?
The mist spreads round, the beam is distant far.
But the light of thy Dar-thula's soul doth dwell
In thee, chief of old Etha great; — but tell,
Son of kind Usnoth, why that broken sigh?
Are we in strange land, son of Etha, aye?"

" These are not rocks of Nathos," he replied,
"And neither is this the roar of his stream wide;
No light from Etha's hall, from this place far.
'Tis a strange land—land of the fierce Cairbar!
The winds are false to us, Dar-thula dear;
Old Erin lifts her shaggy hills but here; —
Althos, up toward the north thou now must go:
Thy steps, Ardan, along the coast, lest foe
In darkness come, and hopes of Etha die.
Toward yonder mossy tower go now will I
To ascertain who near that beam may dwell.
Dar-thula on this shore in peace rest well,

Thou lovely light! for Nathos' sword around
Thee flashes, like the lightning in its wild bound!"

He went; but she there sat alone to hear
The rolling of the wave. The big, salt tear
Falls, as for Nathos now she looks steadfast;
Trembles her soul before the mighty blast!
She turns her ear toward his far off footfall;
That distant tread she hears not now at all.
"Where art thou, oh! where, son of my love?
The wild wind howls around thee and above;
Dark is the hour, but he returns not yet.
What keeps thee, Etha's chief, and have foes met
The hero in the strife of this night black?"
He came—but dark his face as he walked back,
For he had seen his lost friend, loved, well-known;—
'Twas Tura's wall; Cathullin's ghost alone
Stalked there; and from his breast fell frequent sigh;
Terrible the decayed flame of his stern eye!
A column of light mist was his long spear;
And through his dim form did the stars appear;

His voice like the hollow wind in some dark cave,—
His eye like light afar,—grief's tale he gave.
And sad was Nathos' soul as the sun in a day
Of mist, when watery is his face and gray.

"Why, Nathos, dost thou stand sad, mournful there?"
Of him asks Colla's lovely daughter fair.
"A pillar of light unto Dar-thula, thou;
In Etha's chief the joy of her eye is now.
Save Nathos loved, oh, where have I a friend?
My father's, brother's life is at an end!
Upon Seláma's halls doth silence brood;
My land's blue streams with sadness dark are strewed;
With Cormac fell those whom I loved, and all;
In Erin's battles those strong men did fall.
Hear me, O son of mighty Usnoth; hear,
Nathos, my tale of grief so sad and drear.

"Evening darkened upon the plain,—the blue
Streams gliding swift then failed from human view;
While ever and anon the wild blasts strove,
Rustling through the top of old Seláma's grove.

I sat 'neath a tree upon my fathers' wall;
Truthil before my soul passed in death's pall,—
The brother of my love, he who afar
In battle fought against the proud Cairbar.
The gray-haired Colla came, bent on his spear;
Dark was his downcast face, and sorrow drear
Dwelt in his soul.   Upon his side was placed
The sword,—his head his father's helmet graced;
In his strong breast the burning battle grew;
But rising tears he strove to hide from view.

  "'Dar-thula, oh! my daughter!' then he said,
'Thou'rt last of Colla's race,—Truthil is dead!
And toward Selàma's walls Cairbar doth stride
With thousands strong; but I will meet his pride,
Revenging thus my son; but safety where
For thee, Dar-thula, with the dark-brown hair?
Lovely art thou as the sunbeam of Heaven high;
But thy friends are low!'

                   "With bursting sigh,
I said, 'has the son of battle gone—true?
And ceased the gen'rous soul of Truthil through

The field of war to lighten with its glow?
My safety, Colla, then, *is in my bow!*
Father of Truthil dead, the deer I pierce;
Like the desert's hart is not Cairbar fierce?'

"The face of age with joy did then grow bright;
From his eyes crowded tears poured down aright.
The lips of Colla trembled.

      "'Thou art,' said he,
'The sister of Truthil,—in fire of his soul free
Thou burn'st.   Take, Dar-thula, take that spear;
That brazen shield; that burnished helm, spoils here
Of a warrior strong, an early youth's loved son.
As soon as light on Seláma hath begun
To rise, to meet car-borne Cairbar we start;
From shadow of my shield do not depart.
My child, thy father thee could once defend;
But old age trembling doth his hand attend;
And now the strength of his old arm hath failed;—
His soul is dark by heavy grief assailed.'

"In sorrow's shadows drear we passed the night.
But when arose the morning's golden light,

I shone in arms of battle which I bore.

The ancient, gray-haired hero moved before;

Selama's sons stood round old Colla's shield;

Their locks were white, and few were in the field.

The youths with Truthil fell the day before

In car-borne Cormac's bloody battle sore."

 "'"Twas not thus,' said Colla, 'my youth's friends dear,

Ye have long since seen me in arms appear;

When great Confaden fell, not thus I strode

To war. But ye are laden with grief's load;

Darkness of age, like the desert's mist comes on.

My shield is worn with years o'er it long drawn;

My trusty sword is fixed in its own place; *

I told my soul calmness its eve should grace;

Its departure be like to a fading light; —

But the storm again hath come in all its might.

My tottering form bends as an aged oak;

On Selama's walls my boughs are fallen, broke;

---

* In ancient times it was customary for the warrior at a certain age, or when
he became unfit for service, to hang up his arms in the great hall, intending
never afterward to appear in battle; and this stage of life was called " time
of fixing the arms."

I tremble in my place.   O, where art thou,
With thy dead heroes, my loved Truthil, now?
Thou answerest not from out thy rushing blast.
Thy father's soul is sad,—this must not last.
Cairbar, or Colla, one must fall; for I
Feel the returning strength in my arm lie!
My heart leaps wildly at the war's fierce sound.'
   " The hero drew his sword; his people round
Raised gleaming blades, and moved the plain along,
Their gray hair streaming in the high wind strong.
Feasting Cairbar sat.   In still Lena's plain
He saw the coming of the heroes' train,
And called his men to war.   Why should I to
Thee, Nathos, tell how strife of battle grew?
For I have seen thee 'mid a mighty throng,
Like Heaven's lightning swift flashing bright along,
So beautiful, but terrible also,
As mortals in its dreadful course fall low!
Flew Colla's spear, as he recalled again
The battles of his youth.   An arrow then

Whizzed through the air, and pierced the hero's side;
On his echoing shield he fell—and died!
Leaped my soul with fear; mine over him to screen
I stretched; but then my heaving breast was seen!
Cairbar came with his spear; Selàma's maid
He saw, and on his swarthy face joy played;
His lifted steel was stayed.

     He Colla's tomb
Raised, and to Selàma brought me in gloom.
Words of love he spoke, but my soul was sad—
I saw the bucklers which my fathers had;
I saw the sword of car-borne Truthil dear;
I saw the arms of all my dead;—the tear
Was on my cheek. Then didst thou come to me,
Nathos, and oft did saddened Cairbar flee.
As from the morning's beam the desert's ghost
Will flee away, he fled;—far off his host;
And feeble was his arm against thy steel.
Why gloomy, sad, O! Nathos, dost thou feel?"

 "War in my youth I've met," the hero said;
"My arm, when danger first did raise its head,

Could not lift the spear.   But my soul then e'en
Grew bright in presence of the war, as the green,
Narrow vale, when sun his warm beams doth throw,
Before in storm his head he hideth low! —
The lone traveler then mournful joy may feel
As darkness slowly doth itself reveal.
Brightened my soul 'mid danger's cruel stare,
Before I e'en saw thee, Seláma's fair! —
Saw thee like a star that shines o'er hill at night;
Advancing clouds threatening the lovely light!
We're in foes' land,—deceived the winds have thus,
Dar-thula.   Strength of friends is not near us,
Nor Etha's mountains high.   Where shall I find
Peace for the daughter of Colla great and kind.
Nathos' brothers both are brave, and his own
Gleaming sword, too, hath oft in battle shone.
But compared to hosts of dark-brown Cairbar,
What are Usnoth's sons?   Oh! that winds thus far,
Oscar, king of men, had thy sails brought now;
At Cormac's war to be didst promise thou.

Then would my hand be strong as the flaming arm
Of death, and Cairbar shake for fear of harm;
And round Dar-thula peace should never fail.
Heart, why sink? Usnoth's sons may yet prevail."

"And they will prevail, O! Nathos," spoke
The maiden's soul, as it from calm awoke.
"Halls of gloomy Cairbar! Dar-thula ne'er
Shall thee behold.   Those brazen arms hand here,
Which glitter to the meteor passing by;
Them in the dark-bosomed ship I dimly spy.
In battle fierce of steel Dar-thula, too,
Will go.   Ghost of the noble Colla! do
I see thee in that cloud?   And who dim there
Stands by thy side?—the car-borne Truthil fair?—
See halls of him who slew Selárma's chief!
Spirit of my love! no—'tis my belief."

Joy rose in Nathos' face, when he had heard
The fair, white-bosomed maid speak thus her word.

"O! daughter of Selárma, shinest thou
Along my soul!   Come with thy thousands now,

Cairbair!— the strength of Nathos doth return.
O! aged Usnoth, thou shalt never learn
Thy son hath fled.   Thy words on Etha high
I know, when first my sails began to fly
Toward Erin, and toward Tura's walls, then spread.
 " 'Thou goest, Nathos, to the king of shields;' he said,
'Thou goest unto Cathullin, chief of men,
Who ne'er yet from danger fled.   Let not then
Thine arm be feeble, nor have thoughts of flight;
Lest Semo's son say Etha's race are slight.
His words might reach Usnoth's unwilling ear,
And sadden then his soul in his hall here.'
Upon my father's cheek the big tear lay;
He gave this sword;—I came to Tura's bay.
But lo! the halls of Tura silent were.
I looked around, and none to tell was there
Of Semo's generous son.   I went to the hall
Of shells, where hung his fathers' arms, but all
Were gone, and aged Lamhor dropped his tear.
 " 'Whence these arms of steel?' said he, arising near,

‘ Long hath the spear’s light now been absent from

Old Tura’s dusky halls.   From rolling sea ye come?

Or from Temora’s mournful hall ? ’

                                    “ ‘ We come from sea,’

Said I, ‘ from Usnoth’s rising towers;—sons are we

Of Slissáma, Semo’s daughter.   But thou

Son of silent halls, Tura’s chief ’s where now?

Still why should Nathos thus inquire of thee,

For he beholds thy tears,—but tell how he

Did fall, the strong, thou son of Tura lone.

   “ ‘ Like a silent star of night, when it hath flown

Through dark, and is no more,—not thus he fell.

He was like the meteor bright, which doth impel

Itself along into some land afar,

Its course death attending—a sign of war !

Sad are Lego’s banks and streamy Lara’s sound,

Where the son of noble Usnoth struck the ground.’

   “ ‘ The hero fell amid the slaughtering throng;

Ever in battle fierce his hand was strong,’

Said I to him, with a deep and bursting sigh—

‘ Death dimly sat behind his sword e’er nigh.’

" We came to Lego's sounding banks and found
His tomb.   His friends in war were on the ground,
The bards of song.   Three days did we then yield
To grief there;—on the fourth struck I Caithbat's shield.
The heroes gathered round in joy and glee,
Brandishing their beamy spears.   Corlath, the
Friend of car-borne Cairbar, with host was near.
We came as a stream doth in the night appear;
Before us then his heroes fell.

          "And when
The people of the valley came, they then
Saw their red blood the morning's light beneath!
But we rolled away, as the thin mist's wreath,
To Cormac's echoing halls.   Our swords we there
Raised to guard the king; but those halls were bare.
Cormac was dead, and Erin's king no more!
The sons of Erin sadness overbore.
Like clouds which long have threatened rain, then go
Behind the hills, they gloomy now retired slow.
Toward Tura's sounding bay thus in grief drear
Moved Usnoth's sons, and passed Seláma near.

As Lena's mist flees winds did Cairbar flee.
'Twas then that I beheld, Dar-thula, thee,
Like the light of Etha's sun.   'Lovely,' said I,
'Is that beam,' and rose from my breast the sigh.
Fair didst thou come to me, Dar-thula dear,—
But winds have us deceived.   The foe is near!"

   "Yes, near," said Althos in his rushing might,
"On shore I heard the clanging of their arms bright;
I saw the dark wreaths of Erin's standards near.
The voice of Cairbar was distinct and clear,
As loud as Cromla's falling stream.   He'd seen
The dark ship on the sea ere black night, e'en.
His people watch on Lena's dusky plain, and hold
Ten thousand swords."

                    "And let them there," said bold
Nathos, with a smile, "hold their swords, for sure
Usnoth's sons do tremble not at danger's door!
Why with thy foam roll, Erin's roaring sea?
Why do ye rustle on thy dark wings, ye
Whistling storms of sky?   And do ye think, O
Storms, ye keep Nathos on this coast?—ah! no,

His soul detains him, children of the night!
Althos bring my father's arms, which there bright
Thou seest beaming to the stars; and Semo's spear
Also, in the dark-bosomed ship bring here."

The arms he brought, and then did Nathos hide
His limbs in all their shining steel.   The stride
Of the chief was noble: the joy of his eyes
Was terrible; and for Cairbar he spies.
The blowing wind was rustling in his hair.
Dar-thula silent at his side stood there.
She viewed the chief, but strove to hide the sigh;
Yet still the tear swelled in her radiant eye.
   "Althos I see a cave in yon rock bare,"—
Said Etha's chief, "place my Dar-thula there.
And let thy arm my brother be strong now;—
Ardan, we meet the foe, call Cairbar, thou.
May he come Usnoth's son to meet in all
His steel bright;—

                    "Dar-thula, shouldst thou not fall,
Look not on Nathos low;—

13

"Make thy sails stand,
Althos, toward the ringing groves of my own land!
Tell the chief that his son fell with fame;
That his sword did not shun the fight in shame,
So that the joy amid his grief be great;—
Daughter of Colla, in Etha's hall in state
Call the maids there, and let their songs rise then
For Nathos, when Autumn shadowy comes again.
Oh! that the voice of Cona, that Ossian's might
In my praise be heard!—then would my spirit bright
In midst of rushing winds rejoice alway."—

"And thus my voice *shall* praise thee, Nathos, yea,
Chief of the woody Etha!   In thy praise,
Son of Usnoth, Ossian will his voice raise.
Why was I not there at war's first alarm?
Ossian would have died or kept thee from harm!"

We sat in Selma's hall the shell around;
And through the lofty oaks the wind did sound.

Then roared the spirit of the mountain tall,
Touching my harp.   The blast came through the hall,
Like song of the tomb,—the sound was mournful, low.
Fingal first heard, and crowded did his sighs go
From his bosom.
                "Some of my heroes lie
Dead," said the gray-haired king of Morven, " I
The sound of death upon the harp hear now.
Ossian, my son, the trembling strings touch thou.
Bid the sorrow rise, that their loved spirits freed
To Morven's hills with joy may fly in speed."
    I touched the harp before the king,—mournful, soft
Its tone.   "Bend forward from your clouds aloft,"
Said I, "Ghosts of my fathers! lay aside
The terror of your course, as swift ye ride.
Receive now the fallen chief, whether from
A distant land or rolling sea he come.
Place near his robe of mist and cloud-formed spear.
Let a half-extinguished meteor there appear
In shape of this great hero's sword—and oh!
Let now his countenance be lovely so,

That in his presence may delight each friend;—
Bend from thy clouds, ghosts of my fathers, bend!"
Thus sang I to the harp trembling soft and light;—
But Nathos was on Erin's shore in night!
'Mid tumbling waves the foe's voice did he hear;
He silent heard, and rested on his spear.
With light rose morning,—Erin's sons were seen,
Like to gray rocks, with all their trees of green,
They spread along the coast.   Cairbar the while
Stood there, and seeing foes, did grimly smile.
Nathos rushed forward in his strength and might;
Nor could Dar-thula stay behind the fight.
With shining spear she came there by his side.
And who are there in armor and youth's pride?
Who but Usnoth's sons, Althos, and
Dark-haired Ardan?

    "Come Temora's chief, stand
Here now," said Nathos, "and let our fight be
On this coast for the dark-bosomed maid we see.
His people with Nathos are not, but now
Are behind these rolling seas.   Why dost thou

'Gainst Etha's chief bring thousands?   Thou didst fly
From him in battle when his friends were nigh."

"Proud youth! shall Erin's king fight with thee then!
Thy fathers renowned were not, nor kings of men.
Are foes' arms within their halls, or ancient shields?
Cairbar is famed in high Temora's fields;
Nor does he fight with feeble men."   The tear
Started from Nathos.   Toward his brothers near
He turned his eyes.   Their spears at once all flew;
And heroes three lay dead.   Their swords then threw
Their light on high; and Erin's ranks fell back,
As ridge of clouds before the wild wind's track.
His men Cairbar then ordered, and they drew
A thousand bows,—a thousand arrows flew,
Usnoth's sons falling in their blood; like three
Young oaks which stand alone on some hill.   The
Traveler views these fine trees, and wonders how
They grew so lone.   But desert's blast comes now,
Laying them low.   Next day returning there,
He finds them withered and the heath all bare?—

Dar-thula sees them fall, standing in grief drear;
Wildly sad her gaze, although she drops no tear;
Pale is her look; her trembling lips short break
The half-formed words; on the winds her locks do shake.
Gloomy Cairbar came. "Where thy lover now,
Car-borne chief of Etha? Beheld hast thou
Usnoth's halls, or Fingal's dark-brown hills? Yet
If the winds had Dar-thula not thus met,
On Morven e'en my battle soon would roar;
Fingal lie low—grief enter Selma's door!"
Her shield fell from Dar-thula's arm. Appeared
Her fair, white breast, but it with blood was smeared!
An arrow in her side was fixed, and low
She fell on Nathos, like a wreath of snow!
Over his face her flowing hair spreads wide,—
Their blood thus mixes 'round from side to side!

"Daughter of Colla! maiden, low art thou!"
Sang Cairbar's hundred bards. "Broods silence now
O'er Selàma's streams; and Truthil's race
Hath failed. When wilt thou rise in beauty, grace,

Chief of Erin's maids?   Long in the cold tomb
Thy sleep.   In distance far doth morning loom.
The sun shall not to thy bed come and say,
Wake, Dar-thula first of women—'tis day.
The winds of Spring are here.   Upon the hills green
The flowers now shake their heads.   The woods are seen
To wave their growing leaves.

       Sun retire thou!
The daughter of Colla is sleeping now!
For she will not come forth in beauty's dress.
She will not move in steps of loveliness."

A PRAYER FOR MARY.

LINES ADDRESSED TO MY COUSIN,

M. B. S.

O, Mary dear, may each new year
   Shower rich blessings on thy head;
And the deep blue eye of yon soft sky
   Cheerful light upon thee shed!

In a quaint book old a tale is told
   Of a garden rich and bright,
Where Nature's smiles free of all wiles,
   Blossomed sweet in golden light;

Where gay birds flew, of rainbow hue,
    To gladden the ear and eye;
Where placid stream with silver gleam
    Mirrored true the azure sky;

And a joyous pair of creatures fair
    Lived in happiness and love.
Oh! such to thee may this earth be,
    Reflecting yon Heaven above!

And may'st thou long amid love's throng,
    Live to bless and to be blessed;
And wend thy way 'mong rich flowers gay
    To that home of peace and rest.

But should Woe's dart pierce through thy heart,
    And Sorrow her gloom throw o'er,
May angels bright, with wings of light,
    Fan that aching heart and cure!

14

THE OCEAN GRAVE.

FOR MY SISTER M's SCRAP-BOOK.

FAR, far from the land on the vast, mighty deep,
Where the white foaming waves and the grand billows sweep,
With gay streamers sails a good vessel strong,
Far dashing the spray while darting along!
A youth rapt in dream there on the deck lies;
Far absent his thoughts, as sleep seals his eyes.
Away o'er the sea his ship has now sailed;
He has arrived safe, his Lillie has hailed.
And then by her side he thinks he sits there;
Has made her his bride, far absent all care.
Ah! watch how his face all glows with a smile —
He knows not between lies many a mile!
But see the dark clouds; in tumult they fly;
They tell of a storm; they darken the sky.

A few moments since serene was that sky;
And gentle the breeze as soft it stole by;
And placid the sea with its bosom so blue,
A mirror reflecting the clouds as they flew.
Behold! what a change! the winds how they rage,
Like beasts of the woods escaped from their cage!
The white-crested billows, how upward they rise;
Descending again as if from the skies!
The ship like a nut-shell is tossed to and fro,
On old Ocean's bosom now heaving with woe.
The thunders grow louder and roll through the sky,
The lightnings grow brighter and dart from on high!
The winds now are fiercer, and howl o'er the deep,
As the billows roll higher and o'er the ship sweep!
And flies o'er the scene wild Terror sublime;
And tremble the crew—ah! horrible time!

But the Ruler of storms says, "Peace! be ye still."
His word the winds hear, and leave at his will.
The lightnings and thunders then in the sky cease,
And the billows again now slumber in peace;

And the rainbow of Heaven o'erarches the sky;
And Phœbus' bright rays swift fall from on high.
But where that strong ship that flew o'er the deep,
The billows defying, as by they would sweep?
Where that gay vessel that lately sailed there—
That ship with its souls? Mock Echo says, "where?"
In Ocean's dark depths, far, far 'neath the wave,
In the sea's cemetery have hundreds a grave!

The night it is calm, and soft is the air,
When on the sea-shore bends a young maiden fair.
And oh! how angelic, as there she kneels soft!
But hark to her prayer which the breeze bears aloft:

  "Father, sisters, and a mother,
    Thou hast taken all from me;
   In the ocean sleeps my brother,
    Oh! shield Tommie on the sea!"

Alas! she knows not that far 'neath the wave,
Her own dearest Tommie has now found a grave!

In some unfathomed cave in vast ocean deep,
There lonely and cold her lover doth sleep!
From view far concealed, far down in the sea,
His sepulchre white needs the shade of no tree.
Upon his drear, gloomy, mysterious, dark tomb
No flower opening smiles, save the green sea-weed's bloom,
Or the white coral blossoms,—work of a strange race,
The sea's little architects—his tomb to grace.

And that brother, perhaps, there sleeps by his side,
Unroused by sea's roar, unmoved by the tide.

Far from the earth's tumult, calm may they both rest,
Till waked by the last trump in Heaven they are blest!

AN ODE TO

H. W. LONGFELLOW, Esq.

Hail! Poet, thou
Whose noble brow
With diadem is crowned
Of greater beauty, worth
Than any that are found
On heads of kings of earth!

All honor now;—
Indeed art thou
Immortal Burns more like
Than any poet that lives.
His noble heart doth strike
Within thy breast, which gives

To every line
Feeling divine,—
A generous impulse free,—
A sympathy deep, kind.
In thy soul's fount we see
Emotions, thoughts, which find—

As rich they gush
And onward rush,
Like waters from breast deep
Of mother-earth that rise,
And welling up fast sweep—
Welcome in thousand eyes.

Thy blue eye,—fraught
With gems of thought,
Sparkling, serene and bright—
Like miniature view of sky
Cerulean, calm at night,
Spangled with stars, did I

Fancy to be,

As once by thee

I sat, long years past now,

In thy sweet cottage-home

On old Nahant, where thou

Dost love to live and roam.

OLDEN MEMORIES.

ADDRESSED TO MY AUNT, MRS. THOMAS H. SHREVE.

" Behind a frowning providence,
He hides a smiling face."

COWPER.

OH! how ye cling around the soul,
    Sweet olden memories, dearest gems!
As green vines cling around their pole,
    And clustering flowers around their stems.

Ye memories oft are sad but dear,
    Yes, like the rose upon the tomb,
Showing to us that death is near,
    While still it pleases with its bloom.

Oft from thy presence radiant, bright
    E'en as the sun's at day's first dawn,
Our gloom flees off, as ebon night
    Doth flee from him at early morn!

Though ye thy visits oft repeat,
    Oh! welcome! welcome! come again;
For ye do joy for us oft mete;
    As oft do take away our pain.

Upon a still and quiet eve,
    Just when the sun hath sunk to rest,
For lost ones we then love to grieve,
    Although we know that they are blest.

Yes, when "the day has passed and gone,"
    And when "the evening shades appear,"
'Tis then the form of some lost one
    Reflected is in every tear.

And then the form of that one dear,
    Coming in olden memories' vision,
Is, though we seem alone, us near—
    Sweet balm for the heart's incision.

And then rush to us memories olden,
    Dear, happy visions of the past,
Like bright scenes fairy, in dreams golden,
    Scenes far "too beautiful to last!"

As oft round Autumn's setting sun,
    Will glow clouds silver, gold, and blue,
Whose beauty fades, whose glory 's done,
    Before we tire of the rich view.

How many wonder that we are sad,
    When that dear friend 's been long away!
Oh! how can we feel joyous, glad?
    And do they wish us?—We say nay.

Ah! seems the world a stormy ocean,—
　　When a loved one of worth we 've lost—
And on it barks, some for a notion,
　　But others after things of cost.

And very oft to us it seems,
　　That those who strive for the bright goal,
With all their noble spars and beams,
　　Are e'en the first wrecked on the shoal!

But let us not despair, but know
　　That far beneath mad ocean's wave
Rich pearls of worth and beauty glow,
　　And bright dew-drops shine on the grave.

And so behind the dark, gloomy cloud'
　　Sparkles in splendor the smiling star,
Enveloped deep within its shroud
　　'Till the winds blow the mists afar.

Thus oft behind affliction's cloud,
    Where we can only think a frown,
Beams the calm, holy smile of God,
    There mildly on us glowing down!

And then it is old memories dear,
    Like fair, strong cords of silvery light,
Draw off our hearts from all things here,
    Up to high Heaven all glorious, bright.

Then memories sparkling in the eye,
    Thus blinding it to earthly things,
Glow like the meteors in the sky—
    Glow like the light of angels' wings!

Though ye thy visits oft repeat,
    Ye come to us like spirits bright;
Oh! come until our life 's complete—
    Oh! come to cheer us through the night.

AUGUST, 1855.

T O

Wm. C. BRYANT, Esq.

Great poet! when thy free, glorious spirit winged
Its downward flight from Heaven's high battlements,
A bright, immortal spark divine, from the
Unceasing flood which there in brilliancy
Ineffable doth flow, was with it sent,
Which fanned into a glowing flame by wings
Of quick imagination, beams now like
A shining light to guide thy fellow-man,
Who over life's broad sea doth sail, whilst thou
Loom'st up like a tower upon a rocky coast!

Hail! favored child of Nature kind, at whose
Feet thou dost sit, as near a mother dear,
And gaze into her deep, cerulean eye,
And hold with her communion sweet in all

The "visible forms" she doth assume to please
And draw thee close.

              The "various language" which
She speaks, and which so few can understand;
Still thou dost hear, and know, and feel, and then
Tell us that which might otherwise have been
Forever lost.

              But, Poet, come, come—if thou
Hast never seen fair Nature as she doth
To us appear in this our grand old state—
And see our towering mounts, green hills, vast caves,
Majestic streams, our beauteous forests wild,
Illimitable; Nature's fair and blooming
Daughters too; for female loveliness and
Beauty fresh are bright twin-flowers indigenous
To our Kentucky soil.   Come, Poet, come, we'll
Meet thee sure with open Southern hearts and hands.

THE ROSE.

If Zeus chose us a king of the flowers in his mirth,
 He would call to the rose and would royally crown it;—
For the rose, ho, the rose! is the grace of the earth,
 Is the light of the plants that are growing upon it.

Mrs. BROWNING's rendition of
Sappho's Song of the Rose.

WHAT nobler flower

On Nature's bower,

Or in her garden grows?

What sweeter flower

Of magic power

To gladden than the rose?

Before sin came
And endless shame
Upon the earth so fair,
The angels bright
With heavenly light
Were wont to visit there.

Communion sweet,
As then was meet,
They with our parents held ;
And deigned to walk
With them, and talk,
By kindly love impelled.

One lovely day,
When Sol's bright ray
Lit up all Paradise;
And mother Eve,—
I'll not deceive—
Clad in becoming guise

Of innocence
And virtue, whence
Chief loveliness arose;
With her loved lord,
Through Eden broad
Strolled where Euphrates flows,

Two angels fair
The loving pair
Approached thus to address;—
The nobler one,
And higher none,
Spake thus, nor more, nor less:

" Come, brother good,
'Tis meet we should
To-day name every beast
Placed here to roam
In its wide home,—
The greatest and the least."

The other one,
When he had done,
To fair Eve, smiling came:—
  "Come, sister good,
  'Tis meet *we* should,
To all your *flowers* give name."

A look of love,
Like cooing dove
Each to the other threw,
  And parted then,
  I need not pen,
As lovers always do;

Each wishing soon—
Oh! happy boon!—
The other there to meet,
  To tell their love,
  Like cooing dove,—
With word and smile to greet.

We'll Adam leave,
And follow Eve,
Who with her angel-guide,
Walks through her bowers,
Among her flowers,
Sweet objects of her pride.

The Dahlia proud,
Of all the crowd
By far most haughty one;
The Peony red,
With toss of head,
And Heart's-ease full of fun,

With saucy look
From its sly nook;
The Sun-flower bright as flames;
The Violet blue,
The Daisy too,
Had all received their names;

And others too,
Which round them grew,
Had each its name and place,—
Yes, all the flowers
Of Eden's bowers,
But two most full of grace.

The Lily fair
With modest air
Her graceful head inclined,
As they drew near
Her pale as fear,
And name and rank assigned.

But on her right—
Oh! heavenly sight!
There stood a full-blown flower
Of modest mien,
Yet like a queen
Of beauty, grace, and power.

An unfeigned blush,
Like maiden's flush,
Suffused her cheeks with red;
And pride and grace
Sat on her face,
As thus the angel said:—

"Hail! regal Rose!
No flower here grows
So fair, so sweet as thou;
And queenly pride,
And grace beside
Each crowns thy peerless brow.

"And that all now
To thee may bow,
And own thy rule supreme,
O noble Queen,
Of graceful mien,
Thy brow with light shall gleam."

No sooner said,
Than round her head
A halo-glory shone,
As sparks of light
From his wings bright
Around her brow were thrown!

But when man fell—
Ah! sad to tell—
Then disappeared that crown;
Yet still, I ween,
From rank that queen
Was not indeed cast down.

Her primal grace
Adorns her face;
Her regal pride remains;
That noble mien,
Which marks the queen,
Unaltered she retains!

THE NEW-YORK OBSERVER.

HAIL! now,

O thou

Great banner white,

Emblazoned bright

With characters of light

Glowing both day and night!

Long to the breeze thou'st been unfurled

Throughout the vast enlightened world,

Where'er a Christian army strong

With solid phalanx moves along,

In giant, firm, resistless march,

To pass beneath the glorious arch

O'er Zion's wide and golden gate,

Which open its approach doth wait!

Hail! now,

O thou

Herald of Truth,

Bringing to youth,

And aged too,—to all

Who list to hear thy call,

The news,—glad tidings of great joy,

Telling how Christ's followers employ

Their time, their strength; and telling of

His kingdom's progress,—the rule of love.

Herald! in almost every land

Thy spies are there to take their stand;

And thus o'er earth thou hast wide view,

Fearless thy duty e'er to do!

16

TEEDIE AND THE HUMMING-BIRD.

"Mother, what is that darling thing
　　Clad in its rainbow dress;
And with a light and quivering wing,
　　So full of happiness?

"Long have I watched it from my bower,
　　Flying from twig to twig,
And kissing every fragrant flower,
　　Unconscious of fatigue."

"It is a humming-bird, my child,
　　You see so gay and bright,"
The mother fond replied, and smiled
　　To note her child's delight.

"A humming-bird I wish *I* were,
And had two wings so light;
I'd fly about all free from care,
From early morn till night.

"I'd flap my little wings and go
Away up to the sky,
And light upon a cloud of snow,
And sing a song so high!

"And then again to earth I'd fly
To smell the roses sweet,
And place upon your hand so sly
My tiny, little feet!"

"My child, if you the Lord will love,
An angel you shall be;
And two bright, golden wings above
Shall waft you light and free!

"And 'neath God's throne there shall you raise
    Your sweet and silvery voice
In anthems loud of heavenly praise,
    And ever thus rejoice!"

*   *   *   *

A sad and weeping circle stands
    Around a little bed;
A smiling sufferer flaps her hands—
    Her soul to God has fled!

She has a pair of golden wings
    To waft her light and free;
And with a silvery voice she sings
    In endless joy and glee!

*   *   *   *

The mother stands beside the grave
    In which her Teedie lies;
A willow's mournful branches wave
    Before her sobbing eyes.

A humming-bird, with plumage gay,
Lights on her hand in glee;
Then memory fond recalls the day
She wished such bird to be.

Her bright eye sparkles through her tear,
Like sunbeams through the rain;
And then she calls it "Teedie dear,"
And courts it to remain.

It builds its nest upon the bower
O'er Teedie's grave so green;
And oft it kisses every flower
Which smiling there is seen!

THE VISION.

Mrs. M. B. A.

UPON THE NIGHT OF HER MARRIAGE.

DEAR friend, before my eyes one night
A vision passed,—
Strange picture, beautiful and bright
From first to last.
I stood upon a grassy shore,
Where flowers in glee
Their slender forms were bending o'er,
So gracefully,

To bathe their heated brows, and make
  Them cool and white
In waters of a beauteous lake
  Reflecting light
Of skies above.—But while I gazed
  Upon their play,
How much was I surprised, amazed
  To see the spray

Dash high upon the bank of green,
  Followed by wave.
Naught on the lake could then be seen;
  Nor did storm rave.
But soon I saw a boat, all gay
  With streamers bright
And flags and snowy sails, make way,
  Darting in flight

Out from behind a jutting rock;
And in it there
A maiden stood with curling lock,—
Queen-like, bright, fair!
'Twas she the lake from sleep thus woke,
Ruffling its breast;
Radiant as the angel, e'en, who broke
Bethesda's rest,

Coming, like a beam from Heaven's high gate,
To trouble then
Those healing waters, and abate
Suffering of men! —
And then another winged boat,
And others still,
Past me did fly like gulls, or float
Like swans—at will.

In each a gallant man did stand,
    With eye on thee;
To each thou gav'st a smile so bland,
    And full of glee;
While 'mong that little fleet around
    Thy light boat gay
Did spring, as with a living bound
    In merry play.

A smile to each I said,—yes, e'en
    As Nature bright
On mankind all is ever seen
    The golden light
Of her sunny countenance to throw;
    Though in her gaze,
To him, who loving most doth show
    It best always,

Encouragement most marked gives she.—
So 'twas with one,
Who e'er was close by side of thee,—
His life, his sun.
He asked thee in his light bark near
Thyself to place;
And thus with him to sail fore'er.
And from thy face

A joyous smile 'mid conscious blush
Thou didst him send;
As sun-beam bright with crimson flush
Of eve doth blend!
The hero of the manly form
Did woo thee more;
He said he'd fear no wave or storm,
Whilst thee he bore;

But that together both would sail
In happiness;
And neither would the other fail
In all distress.—
I heard no more, for summer breeze
Did rustle through
The waving boughs of dark green trees,
Which on shore grew.

But soon I saw thee, maiden fair,
Step in his boat;
Nor need I tell how on thee there,
His eye did dote.
Each face was lit with pleasure's ray—
Each was joy's throne.
But by soft winds from sight away
That boat was blown.

And, now, dear friend, thou dost within
Love's gay bark light
The matrimonial voyage begin,
On the river bright
Of life, with one thou lov'st.—May skies
Smile e'er on each,
Like light which falls from angels' eyes,
Till Heaven ye reach!

TO MISS E. P.

My friend, through thy heart ever flow
All blithe, clear, and free as they go,
Joy's streams, their bright currents there pouring;
In merriment loud and gay roaring
Like wild Minne-ha-ha's mirth-sound,
As deep, laughing waters there bound!

And round thy cheek's fresh bloom so fair
May ever be seen clustering there
Light, sunny smiles bright, thus arraying
Themselves in mild beauty while staying;
And dropping with soft, tiny feet,
On lips always rosy and sweet,

To sip the dew which they distill,—
To get on such dainty food fill;
As round the rich flowers ever flying,
Or on their soft petals there lying,
Are golden-winged butterflies bright
Their honey to suck in delight!

THE LAST VICTIM OF THE DELUGE.

AGES of years

With smiles and tears

Had passed away

Since that first day,

When God's great Spirit moved along

Upon the water's face, and he

Divided there by his hand strong,

The dark from light, and land from sea;—

Since God man made

And on him laid,

In grace and love,

The impress of

His beauteous image, with the stamp

Of his all-glorious Godhead great;

And gave him conscience—that bright lamp

Of Truth, to guide in his free state.

At time we pen

Of, hordes of men

Cover the land,

As shells the strand.

But though the shells, in still small voice,

Of God soft whisper in man's ear,

Not in the Lord does *he* rejoice,

Hating the One who placed him here.

But his God now,

When he sees how

Man's every thought

With sin is fraught,

Repents him sore that he has made

And placed this creature on the earth,

Since he has sinned and disobeyed

Unto this day from his first birth.

His fiat loud

From cloud to cloud,

Like thunder runs,

Or boom of guns,

Till reaching earth it scatters wide

Fear, consternation, horror, dread,

Among these hearts so full of pride,

Fearing what God in wrath has said:—

" Ye me defy!

Ah! all shall die

’Neath the flood’s wave,

Nor one shall save

His life but Noah and his household,

Who in an ark shall safe there ride,

Nor fear the billows strong and bold—

Our-pourings of my wrath defied!”

And then black Death

Breathing hot breath,

On his horse pale,

Followed by trail

Of fire and smoke and all hell glad,

In blazing pomp, terror sublime,

Rides through the skies, where all earth bad

And vile can view—ah! awful time!

The demon, Storm,

Shows his dark form;

The lightnings thick

Pierce clouds, and quick

They burst; and all "the windows of

Heaven are opened," and waters pour

In torrents strong down from above;

And "fountains of the great deep roar!"

The wild winds fly;

The waves toss high;

The thunder rolls,

And man's knell tolls;

And drear, black Darkness darkly frowns

And wraps the world in a cloud of gloom,

A sable pall, which thus surrounds

These blind, benighted sinners' tomb!

Black is the sky;

Black waves roll high;

Black demons fell,

Escaped from hell,

Fly through black earth; while black despair

Sits on men's countenances dark;

And on black hearts' thrones ebon there

Black Sin doth reign; nor shines hope's spark.

The waters rise

Up toward the skies,

Thus sweeping all

From housetop tall,

From pinnacle and spire and hill;

From tree and mountain too, as wild,

Their raging billows roll, until

Has perished man and woman, child;—

Till have met death

All who by breath

Did keep their life,

Before in strife

Of these mad elements they died;

Save one gigantic, mighty man

Who, beating hard the waves aside,

Will, if in human strength he can,

Reach a rock near,

Which he sees rear

Itself alone;

For there is shown

No other eminence, whose head

Still stands above this raging sea,

This mighty tomb of all earth's dead,

Kings, beggars, rich, poor, bond, and free!

Yes, all have died

In sin and pride,—

Have died because

God's holy laws

They mocked, nor feared to scorn his power;

By thousands, hundreds, tens, and then

But one by one, whilst Death did lower.

And he of all the race of men

Alone is left,

Of friends bereft.

Bravely he beats

Each wave he meets,

And struggles hard to reach that rock.

But see! he uses but one arm.

And has the other in tempest's shock

Met with some accident and harm?

Ah! hard to be

Cast on such sea,

And whirled along,

E'en if he strong

Were in each limb; but with one maimed,

Oh! doubly so.—Or in a sling

Was it placed ere the deluge lamed?

It is tied with *affection's string!*

Behold! close pressed

Against his breast

He clasps his boy,

His only joy!

Wife, mother, father, sisters, friends,

In the gulf of wrath have all been lost.

He 'mong their corpses his way wends,

With one child left, on billows tossed!

One feeling mild

These waters wild

From his dark soul,

As mad they roll,

Cannot wash out, nor lessen e'en.

One soft emotion lingers still;—

For no man wholly vile is seen,

Though he may lie, and steal, and kill,

And curse his God,

Nor fear his rod;

Hate every man,

And lead the van

Of evil-doers fell in crime.—

This sinful man still loves his child,

And here presents a scene sublime!

Alas! that such hath God reviled.

"Ah! if I yet
By toil may get
Upon that high
Rock to me nigh,
I there may save my life, and thine,
My child!" Poor man! thou dost not know
That both these lives thou must resign.
As all have gone ye two must go!

He reaches now,
With aching brow
And leaping heart
And eyes which start
With tears of joy, this rock, which rears
Itself full thirty feet above
The raging flood; and less his fears
For self and boy—child of his love.

13

On top of it

He now doth sit

Himself to rest,

So long oppressed

By care, fatigue; and then the head

Of his loved boy he lifts, and smiles.

But no smile answers his; he 's—dead!

"'Tis false, yes, 'tis but fancy's wiles,"

In grief he cries,

"Come, ope thy eyes,

My boy; thou art

Not dead; thy heart

Still beats, I know."—But yet he feels

Life 's gone, and o'er his soul to pass,

As some cold reptile slowly steals,

Dread consciousness 'tis so, alas!

But still he 's pressed
Close to his breast.
A tear from eye,
From heart a sigh;
And for the first time then his head
He raises up, and takes a view,
Casting his gaze o'er all the dread
Expanse of waters black and blue,

Or foaming white
Like spectres light,
As they fly past,
All leaping fast.
Oh! terribly sublime the sight!
Oh! awfully magnificent,
And wildly grand!   Was such a night
Of desolation ever sent

Upon this earth,

To drown its mirth;

Or other world,

Where all was hurled

In one great yawning chasm wide,

Of ruin and destruction vast ;

Its habitants with all their pride,

Their sins, their woes, joys, pleasures cast

In this gulf deep

By God's wrath's sweep ?—

If such a one

Rolls round the sun

As this revolving globe of ours.—

Yes, what a scene for him here then,

As there he sits, when all the powers

Of Heaven and Earth and Hell 'gainst men

Seem thus combined,—

'Gainst these poor, blind,

Weak creatures vile,

Laden with pile

Of sins and errors black, so great

And heavy that they could not bear

Up under this such onerous weight,

But 'neath the flood sank in despair!

As far as eye

Can straining spy,

He sees waves and

High billows grand;

Seas, oceans, waters, waters, naught

But waters dark, save here and there

A floating house, or tree, plank, caught

In maelstroms wild, as on they tear

In whirls around

With hoarse, harsh sound.

Or then he may

See far away,

Or near perhaps, now cold and dead,

Some human form, whose snowy shroud

Is foaming wave, and whose death-bed

Was this vast sea—for humble, proud!

And now appears,

As high it rears

Itself above

The level of

This deluge great, the Ark, which floats

In safety past, but far away.

Its ride secure o'er seas he notes;

But not one single, glistening ray

Of wakening light
Then gilds his night,—
The cloud of gloom,
Which like a tomb,
Now holds his buried hopes drowned, dead,
As he in fear sees rising fast,
In their approach so wild and dread,
Up toward his seat these waters vast;

And too well knows
That none but those,
Who through the strife
Preserved dear life,
Placed in the Ark, need expect there
Thus safe to ride: and then his back
He turns in absolute despair,
And blacker grows his gloom-cloud black!

But still there is

Not yet on his

Face any sign,

Or faint outline

Of sorrow for transgression fell,—

Contrition and repentance meek.

Such words his firm lips do not tell.

That countenance doth but bespeak

Rebellion still,

Pride and self-will.

His thoughts of sin,

Hidden within,

Behind his heart's strong castle-walls

Their first resolve maintain yet firm,

Nor harken to contrition's calls,

Surrendering arms upon *no term!*

Should strong waves sweep

Into the deep

Him soon, once more

He'll battle o'er

Their barriers high, and strive to gain

Some house, or raft, tree, floating still—

Position which he will maintain,

In his defiance mad, until—

He knows not when.—

Past human ken

The heart's stern pride,

God, man, defied,

As wickedly it oft hath done.

Poor man! that stern resolve still there

Is Satan's offspring, his own son,

Or blind resolve of black despair! —

But see cast there,
With bosom fair,
And soft face mild,
On billows wild
A female form!   Up toward him now
The wave bears it in its swift route,
Those raven curls from snowy brow
Thrown back, in graceful trail spread out!

Behold him sit
There watching it
As it doth come.
But, hark! now from
His heaving breast, a piteous sigh
Is cast on winds that whistle past,
And then a wild and shrill, loud cry
Doth pierce the air like clarion's blast!

"My wife! my wife!

In this mad strife

Of winds and rain

Thou hast been slain!

Arouse! my babe, my sleeping child!

And see thy mother dead and cold,

Tossed here on billows dark and wild,—

She who to breast thee loved to fold!"

Again he cries,

"Come, ope thy eyes

My boy; thou art

Not dead; thy heart

Still beats, I know."—Again he feels

Life's gone, and o'er his soul to pass,

As some cold reptile slowly steals,

Dread consciousness 'tis so, alas!

And then clear o'er

His heart-stream's shore

Doth wildly roll,

Flooding his soul,

A deluge of agony intense.

Weak Reason from her throne falls then,

Fierce, raging Madness driving hence,

By Satan sent from her hell-den;

By Beelzebub,

Who cannot rub,

In perfect glee

And ecstacy,

His brawny hands, while one remains

Upon the earth from him still free!—

Yes, o'er his mind wild Fury reigns—

Poor man! a raving maniac he!

His boy long pressed
Close to his breast
Though cold and dead,
Is dropped in dread
And raging jaws of gulf beneath.
He grasps some sea-weed flying by;
He twists of it a royal wreath,
And puts it on his white brow high.

He thinks that he
Sits o'er Hell's sea;
His rough, cold stone
A regal throne,
Whose occupant is no less than
His great Satanic Majesty!—
Ah! poor, deluded, crazy, man!
When Reason 's gone 'tis sad to *be*.

And when the wave

His foot doth lave,

As rising high

These waters fly,

He from the whirlpool jerks an oar;

And jumping up in rage he shouts,

"Aback! my slaves; why do ye pour

Thy ranks toward me with mocking flouts!

"Do ye rebel,

Demons of hell!

With this my spear,

Which I hold here,

I'll pierce each heart! I warn thy bands."

And as he speaks and makes air ring,

With regal mien he proud there stands,

And full eight feet—a giant king!

But waters still
Rise, rise until
The rock whereon
He stands is gone
From view, and they thus quite submerge
His feet, which, in his weary cruise,
Made wet and chilled in wave and surge,
Are paralyzed and action lose.

As he mad raves,
And thinks these waves
Are demons fell
Of his own Hell,
In insurrection rising now
'Gainst him, their lawful king well-known,
To snatch his crown off from his brow,
And dispossess him of his throne,

He shouts aloud,

As he stands proud,

"All ye, aback!

Ye devils black!

Thy foaming jaws I swear I'll pierce

With my strong spear; though ye have tied

My royal feet, ye demons fierce,

Free still my arm, and ye defied!"

With giant might

Hell's king in fight,

As fiends move near,

Thrusts with his spear,

Which deep is plunged—in the breast cold

Of his dead wife—by billows slain!

He thinks from the insurgents bold

The gore which now that oar doth stain!

"Demons of hell,

Do ye rebel!

I 'll make thy blood

Flow like a flood!—

Se ye my squadron coming near!

Not one of all shall save his life!"—

Poor man! think'st thou this great ark here

Thy fleet to help thee in thy strife?

The devils heed

Him not—in speed

They climb about

His throat with shout

Of curse and jeer. "Think ye," he cries,

"Think ye to choke thy lord and king!

Above thy heads my arm yet flies,

Destruction on ye all to bring!"

19

With roar and frown

They dash his crown

From his proud brow,

And even now

His spear they snatch from his strong hand.

Deep in the gulf their king is hurled!

And in their triumph wild and grand

They revel o'er a conquered world!

All off are swept,

And none are kept,

Save in Ark those

Whom there God chose!

Then blacker still black Darkness frowns,

And wraps the world in a cloud of gloom—

A sable pall which thus surrounds

These blind, benighted sinners' tomb!

To C. and O.

May Fortune strew
Your pathway through
This fleeting life
Of joy and strife,
With sweetest flowers
From her rich bowers!—
And no thorns pierce
With their teeth fierce,
Or misery's darts,
Your throbbing hearts!
Adown life's stream,
'Neath joy's bright beam,

In bonds of love

Like those above—

Like angels feel,

As "true as steel,"

E'er may you glide

Thus side by side,

In light barks free

Of destiny,

Until you reach

That radiant beach

Where spirits sport—

Heaven's own bright port!

August, 1858.

TO

Mrs. S. A. WORTHINGTON,

OF CINCINNATI.

My Aunt, a merry Christmas now!
   A happy Christmas-day
To gild with light thy noble brow,
   Like crown of diamond ray;
While joy's bells are gaily ringing,
   Sending through thy own loved home
   Sweet chimes from the crystal dome
   Of the temple of thy heart,
Memories there, like ivy, clinging
   To its walls too tight to part; —

The temple of thy heart, whose doors
    Are ever open wide,
Thus bidding all thy friends by scores
    To come, and there abide,
With thy spirit bright communing;
    There to love and sympathize:
    There to let their voices rise
And re-echo through its aisles,
With thy music's notes attuning,—
    Bright their faces with love's smiles!

Now though within this structure fair
    There are some vacant seats,
Showing us cruel Death e'en there
    Now and then his stroke repeats,
Cutting down some flower in beauty,
    Striking cold some dear, loved friend,
    Whose life seemed with thine to blend;
    While on the wall on tablet white,
Thou, performing sacred duty,
    An *In Memoriam* dost write:—

Yes, though that edifice hath oft
   With mourning's curtains hung,
While snowy angels' foot-falls soft,
   Like steps of Sorrow, rung
Along the marble floors so slowly,
   As they bore some cherished form
   To their home beyond earth's storm.
   Far beyond our "vale of tears"—
To their Eden bright and holy,
   There to live through endless years : —

Though oft along that silent nave
   Sad choral strains have rolled
Their mournful, low, resounding wave,
   As requiem those bells tolled,
Deep and solemn as the roaring
   Of old Ocean, when the surge
   On his harp sounds funeral dirge
   Over those just wildly tossed,
Giant Tempest his breath pouring
   On their ship until 'twas lost : —

Still, Aunt, a merry Christmas now!
  A happy Christmas-day
To gild with light thy noble brow,
  Like crown of diamond ray;
While joy's bells are gaily ringing,
  Sending though thy own loved home
  Sweet chimes from the crystal dome
Of the temple of thy heart,
Memories there, like ivy, clinging
  To its walls too tight to part!

Be it like some Cathedral grand,
  In fair Italia's clime,
Which a monument doth stand
  Of ages past—of time;
'Neath whose floors the dead are sleeping;
  For whose loss hath organ rolled;
  For whose death the chime hath tolled;
  But now some holiday is there
Festoons from each arch are sweeping,
  As gay music stirs the air!

Dear Aunt, when I look back, along
   The bright, green avenue
Of my past life, 'neath whose vault song
   Of happiness oft flew,
With its merry note resounding;
    Where not oft a mournful lay,
    With its heavy wing, would stray,
    I hear gay and youthful strains
Of love for thee therein light bounding
    On feet silvery in glad trains!

I love thee still, and wish thee now
   A happy Christmas-day
To gild with light thy noble brow,
   Like crown of diamond ray;
While joy's bells are gaily ringing,
    Sending through thy own loved home
    Sweet chimes from the crystal dome
    Of the temple of thy heart,
Memories there, like ivy, clinging
    To its walls too tight to part!

THE HALLS OF MEMORY.

My Friend, oh! often doth the avenue
Of the long Past appear a temple great
To me, and every tree in lengthy row
Along the road o'er which I traveled once
Becomes a marble column, which supports
A graceful arch o'erhead; and on each side,
The intermediate space filled by the sky
Then seems a panel great, transparent, clear
As glass, while here and there rich, rainbow-tinted
Clouds from heaven high throw their reflections bri>
Filling the apertures with gothic windows
Gilt with all the septenary colors of
God's glorious sun.

             And then the whole transformed
Beneath imagination's light—as once
Were wont to rise, at the bright and magic flash
Of young Aladdin's lamp, grand palaces—
Is seen a picture-gallery great, on whose
High, polished walls hath Memory painted there,
With skillful hand, those scenes, events, and deeds,
Which she, e'er thoughtful of the Future, thus
Records for our own retrospective view.
And there with artful brush hath she drawn forms
(Like shadows true, but brighter, fuller far)
Of friends, acquaintances, not often seen,
Or not for a long time, or dead perhaps;—
Yes, it may be of those whom once I knew,
Admired and loved; and whose corporeal shapes
Would long ago from mind have passed had not
This artist kind preserved them thus for me.
And round such she hath drawn broad, ebon bands,
Like mourning crape wreathed round our pictures dear.

    'Tis true that some have almost faded out,

And these Imagination must renew
By filling up their naked lineaments
And features indistinct ; for Memory
Doth not like us to neglect her works, and
Seldom will she paint again what we have
Thus abused by letting Time with his strong
Hand deface, or rub entirely out, the
Labors of her brush.

     But there are many yet—
Bright pictures, which will visible remain
And plain, as long, perhaps, as life shall last.
And these among a portrait there full-length,
I see, of one whom all who knew her loved,—
My mother's *dearest friend !*

       Thence gazes she,
As down I pass along these silent halls,
Standing erect, with noble mien, in all
Her native majesty, a very queen ! —
No potentate at whose *pride-swollen*
Feet, so tender that they scarce may touch the
Earth contemned, bows some vast race abject and low—

But a proud sovereign true, KENTUCKY-BORN!
That eye is still undimmed; and pictured there,
As on a crystal plate, sits strong Resolve
Embracing gentle Love!

                  Her name I need
Not call, for thou dost recognise her, on
Whose breast an infant thou didst oft-times lie
In sweet repose, rocked in the cradle of
Her arms by heavings of that bosom, which
Swelled with her yearning love; and gently soothed
By beatings of that kind and noble heart
That sounded o'er soft lullabies.

                    My Friend,
Wouldst thou approach as near pefection as
A woman may? Then strive to imitate
All of those virtues and those graces which
Did ever her adorn, as with a robe
Of honor such as women few have worn!

CAPTIVES OF BABYLON.

A VERSIFICATION OF THE 137TH PSALM.

By Babylon's rivers dark
　　We sat us down; and wept
When we thought of Zion's park,
　　Where God our flock once kept!

And our plaintive harps we swung
　　Upon the willows' boughs,
Whose low heads in sorrow hung,
　　As emblems true of ours!

For e'en they who led us thus
   Away from our own land
Demanded a song of us—
   A sad and captive band!

How shall we the Lord's song sing
   In this a foreign land?
How can we the voice make ring—
   A sad and captive band?

Jerusalem! my loved home dear,
   If I forget thee, may
Then my own right hand lose e'er
   Its cunning that same day.

If I do not think of thee,
   Let cleave to the roof of
My mouth my tongue;—if thou be
   Not my chief joy above.

Remember, O Lord, we pray,
  The children of Edom, who,
In Jerusalem's mournful day,
  Said, " rase it—blot from view!"

O daughter of Babylon, who
  Shall be destroyed thus,
Happy be he who doth do
  As thou hast done to us!

Ah! happy shall that man be,
  Who takes thy little ones,
And dashes them angrily
  Against the rough, hard stones!

ODE TO

W. D. GALLAGHER.

My lay I pray
　　Thee now to hear—
My song not long
　　Though theme be dear.
Why, art thou silent, still so long
Thou sweet Meonian bird of song?
Why, poet-warbler of the west?
Art sick?—hang'st head upon thy breast?
Like wet bird's chilled droopest thy wing?
And doth Misfortune her lead-weight bring,
And place upon thy throbbing heart,
And press till streams of woe thence start?
We miss thee: warbler, sing again
So sweetly unto listening men

And women, children anxious all
To hear through grove and vale thy call.
'Twill lighten both thy heart and ours,
Enchanting us in silent hours.
Come carol now, let thy notes dear
'Mong old Kentucky's hills there e'er
Flow on in bright and silvery stream
Sparkling all o'er with diamond gleam;
Now dashing fast, and leaping wild;
Now tripping on like merry child;
Now roaring like the swollen brook;
Now stealing soft as spring from nook,
But ever pleasing, wakening us;—
Oh! chant, and warble, carol thus!
Long years ago thou didst thus sing,
And still thy clarion notes do ring
Reverberating 'mong the hills,
And answering back the babbling rills; —
Yes, ever pleasing, wakening us; —
Oh! chant, and warble, carol thus!

THE WHITE ANGEL.

And now the soft foot-fall of the young creature as she swept quietly along, and the gleam of the torch-light on her white figure, which caused her, apparently, to stand forth alone from the darkness, sent a thrill through the young man; for she seemed to him like a white angel gliding through the church. * * * * * And now the organ began to reveal its noblest resources, the white church-angel, all the while, looking dreamily on, with the same smile of unworldly sweetness in her face.

Extracts from a private memoir of his wife, by R. STORRS WILLIS.

THIS LITTLE POEM IS DEDICATED TO LITTLE ANNIE, BLANCHE, AND JESSIE W.

THE dew-drop with its diamond eye
Glitters awhile then off doth hie,
Like to the humming-bird, which from
Its hidden nook will sometimes come
To gladden with its plumage bright,
And then fly off like a beam of light!—
The rainbow with its varied hue
Delights us with a passing view,

Sky spanning, a triumphal arch
Beneath which unseen legions march
Of happy angels in glad trains,
Singing hosannas in sweet strains ;
Praising their King for the promise, which,
In his kind mercy and grace rich,
Made to his children here below,
Is stamped by that great seal—his bow.
But man can have but fleeting glance
At Heaven ; and before advance
In sight these glorious legions fair
The cloudy curtains drop, lest stare
Of mortal beings should peer through—
See things unfit for carnal view.—

The graceful, regal, heart-loved rose,
The sweetest flower on earth that grows,
Greets with its bloom a few, short days,
Then pines and withers, falls, decays.

Know you a gentle creature who
Round her doth e'er soft radiance strew,—
Like Phœbus calm, serene and bright—
"With something of an angel's light;"
With scarce a frown or look demure,—
A being gay and happy, pure
As snow-flake which on milk-white wing
From sky to earth itself doth bring?
Do you know such and love?—ah! hark,
Upon her brow Death's mystic mark
Is placed. Not long will she remain;
Of Heaven such;—to hope were vain.
I have just read of one like this—
One whom asleep would angels kiss,
Their sister sent from her bright home
Upon the earth awhile to roam—
In sweet memorial from the hand
Of one with whom in this strange land
She shared, a few, short, happy years,
Her hopes and pleasures, joys and tears.

I should have known, had he not said,
That form was laid among the dead;
She could not long stay here below,
Her sisters calling her to go.
The fair, white angel bade farewell
To those who knew and loved her well;
And mantled in pure robes—no *shroud!*—
She flapped her pinions bright.   Through cloud
And air she flew, until she stood
At Heaven's gate, whose keeper good
Thew open wide his portals, and
Welcomed her with a brother's hand!

Oh! grieve not, children dear, grieve not;
Your mother's garments bear no spot
Of sin; but white as falling snow
Their graceful folds around her flow.
A golden harp she holds in hand,
Singing sweet anthems with the band
Of sister angels round God's throne,
In rich, melodious, rapturous tone!

But still she has you e'er in view
And prays and intercedes for you;
And hopes with yearning heart the day
May be as yet not far away
When you shall meet her there above;
In each eye sparkling joy and love.

But though called from her loved ones here
She fled unto her Saviour dear,
Still when your angel-ma through sky,
In her long heavenward flight did fly,
She left a rich and sparkling light
To gild your souls throughout the night,—
Not like the glow-worm's feeble spark,
A moment flashing on the dark;
Nor like the comet whose blaze dies,
And flees off quickly from our eyes;—
But like a luminous, bright star
It shines on you, but not afar!
And every cloud of sorrow drear
That like a pall falls round you e'er,

Its glistening rays will light and tinge,
Surrounding with a golden fringe!
Then this be e'er your hope and prayer,
That God of you will take good care,
And guide your barks o'er life's wild sea,
Until you reach high Heaven's bright lee,
And twine your arms around neck of
Your angel-ma in sky above!

To Mrs. C. S.

A perfect woman, nobly planned,
To warn, to suffer, and command.

WORDSWORTH.

O LOVELY, honored queen
Of noble, regal mien,
Before thy throne are bending
Thy subjects, oft prayers sending
Up through the azure sky,
Which like winged angels fly,
All bright and holy kneeling
'Neath mercy-seat, with feeling
And earnestness implore
God on thee blessings pour;—

Say, lovely, honored queen
Of noble, regal mien,
How dost thou rule these bending,
While heavenward their prayers sending?
 With sceptre true of love
 Strong as that which, above,
Her realms fair Venus swaying,
Ruled gods and men obeying.
 Thus do thy friends' hearts bow
 Before thee gladly now.

 Once, chroniclers relate,
 A dame of wealth and state,
(From fair Campania hailing,)
But with a *womanine failing!*
 Before Cornelia laid
 Her gems and pearls displayed.
The Roman matron smiling
And chatting, time beguiling
 Until her children dear
 From school returned, said: "Here

My ornaments these bright!"
Maternal pride, delight!—
Kind Fortune oft caressing
Hath heaped on thee rich blessing.
Thou art a mother fond,
Tied with affection's bond.
In thy crown of joy glowing
Like the comet, its rays throwing,
Thou hast bright jewels rare;
These thy loved children fair!

And then withal thou art
A woman of gentle heart.
Its sympathy deep wooing,
(As dove wins dove by cooing,)
Draws with its plaintive voice,
Making friends' hearts rejoice.
Thy face is ever beaming,
With radiant, soft light gleaming
From that warm soul of thine,
As sky 'neath sun doth shine!

ODE TO

GEO. D. PRENTICE, Esq.

Hail, Poet! we
Would speak to thee;
With grateful hearts thus thanking now
For all the melody which thou
Hast given e'er,
To us who hear.
But still we chide, because not more
Thou lett'st its sparkling waters pour!

Our bosoms swell,

Oft as we dwell

Upon the thoughts and sentiments

Thy poetry to our minds presents,

Whilst breathing fire—

That doth inspire

With feelings kindred unto thine—

Lit with a glowing spark divine,

In Heaven high caught,

And to thee brought

By thy own guardian angel bright

To gild thy soul with meteor light,

Reflected thus

Warmly on us,

As on revolving planet rays

Of Sol e'er fall like comet's blaze!

But why not now,

Poet, dost write thou

As once of old in times gone past?

Shall not thy fires of genius last?

Do not refuse

To court thy muse,

Lest wearied out she takes her flight

To Heaven whence she came in light!

What wouldst thou say,

If told to-day

Of one e'er wont to cull and cast,

In Norway's maelstrom whirling fast,

Flowers, fairest, best,

And then protest

That its waves with their wrath and roar

Could not hurt them as round they tore!

With great surprise,

"He were not wise,"

Sure thou would'st say, "who thus would act,

And thus could think;"—and it were fact.

"Thou art the man!"

Thy conduct scan.

Thy blossoms, buds poetic, all

In such strange place thou dost let fall!

They wildly thrown

Are thickly strown

In the political whirlpool,

Where Strife, Contention, Terror rule;

There fiercely tossed,

Forever lost!

'Tis wrong,—the earth needs their rich bloom,

Thy fellow-men need their perfume!

Oh! leave the world,

Where they are whirled;

Seek Nature's solitudes and groves,

And hills, and vales, where Poesy roves,

Where Heaven's cool dews

May them suffuse,

And bright sun warm, until they grow

As sweet as any here below!

Let there the bird

Of song be heard,

Which dwells within thy throbbing heart,

Whose voice again may wakening start,

Hearing the call

Of warblers all,

Who frequent e'er these quiet nooks,

And sing unto the babbling brooks.

Its note too oft,

Gentle and soft,

Or ringing out clear, loud, and gay,

Has not been heard, else thrown away

Amidst the toil,

And wild turmoil,

Confusion, strife, and noise of earth,

As if not loved, and nothing worth!

OMNIBUS EST MORI.

I SOMETIMES dream—unfortunate the man
Who when in slumber held ne'er feels that he
Doth move, and act, and think, clothed in the noble
Majesty of thought and being; whose mind,
While body rests, is always wrapped in dead
And *mummifying* lethargy, no more
To stir till wakened by the light of day;
Just as the reptile e'en, that drags his cold
And sluggish length into the crevice of
Some shattered rock, and dormant lies until
From sleep aroused by Spring's warm, genial smile—
Unfortunate such mortals are, if such

There be, except perhaps the bloody man
Whose bloody hands are stained with gore of him
Whom he hath offered on the altar of
His vengeance dire, or envy, avarice,
To please the demon, who makes his hard heart
Of stone into a throne, whereon she sits
And rules supreme, his queen; or some other
Villain, who, wearied in mind all day by
Gloomy thoughts of gloomy deeds, would fain wish, when
His body rests, to bathe his fevered soul
In Lethe's cool and soothing stream, fearing
The nightmare horrible, which oft would make
"Each separate hair to stand on end."

         But, thou,
O, Christian dreamer, for "wealth of Ormus or
Of Ind," wouldst thou forfeit this boon which God
To thee has given—the power to waft thy soul
In lightning-flight, upon the rapid wing
Of bright imagination, escaping for
The time from its frail tenement "of earth.

Earthy," which here imprisons it, and—like
Some eagle proud bursting from his dark cage—
Soaring aloft, until it reaches, e'en,
The golden gates of Heaven, beholding there
Such scenes as John on Patmos saw—such scenes
Glorious and bright, as none but angels see
In glorious, bright, reality?

      Wouldst lose this
Boon, Musician, thou, who mayst catch oft, when
With his sable wing kind Morpheus hath thee fanned
And lulled to sleep, such strains of melody
As thou perhaps canst never hear in a long
Lifetime from a human instrument—strains from
The harp some spirit strikes unseen?

        And, thou,
O, Artist, who mayst view such scenery, thus,—
Such pictures grand as have been placed within
"This universal *frame*,"—reflections bright
Of which on canvas of the mind are drawn
With magic art by Fancy's skillful hand,
Invisible.

And thou, O, Poet divine,
Through channels of whose fervid soul, then, often flow
Those sparkling streams of thought and sentiment,
Of feeling, song, perhaps oft brighter much
Than thou awake may feel, thy body, then,
Upon the gushing fountains of the heart
Not weighing down, like a heavy clod of clay—
An incubus restraining, or, may be,
Polluting with its dross the waters clear,
Too oft, when thou awake wouldst wish them on
To flow, free, unrestrained, in torrents pure;—
Say, wouldst thou for a miser's fondled bane—
The golden bird, that will, more tightly pressed,
But eat, the more, his dwindling, bloodless heart;—
Say, wouldst thou for a Shylock's hoarded wealth,
Who snatches at each glittering speck he sees,
"Unlocks his gold, and counts it till he dies,"
Forfeit such boon?

And thousands, millions yea,
Whom Nature, as these named, hath favored not,

Do prize, esteem, and love the heavenly gift
Of dream!—

         I have just dreamed; and what a dream!
"Half light, half shade," half smile, half frown.   I saw
A gloomy giant-form, emaciate
And grim—a ghastly, awful skeleton,
With drapery naught save waving clouds of black,
That hung around like folds of mourning crape.
And darker than this sable cloud he bore
A banner marked with letters far more black.
"OMNIBUS EST MORI," thereon I read,
In characters as dread and drear as those
The unseen hand of God once wrote upon
The scroll of heavens asunder widely torn,
When floods of rain gushed forth and hid the earth!

  Adown the floor of some long hospital,
Where ranged on either side were beds, in each
Of which methought some sufferer lay—a man
Or woman, child;—adown this avenue,

Which to a graveyard seemed at last to lead,
I saw the silent, gloomy, awful march
Of silent, gloomy, awful DEATH!

His frown
I thought grew blacker still; his banner great
Seemed 'neath its ebon shade now blacker too,
As he approached a bed whereon there tossed,
Like wave of ocean mad, a man in pain
And agony intense.

He saw dread DEATH
Draw near; and fear and terror wild flew o'er
His trembling face, as e'en birds fly and cast
Their shadows dark upon the troubled sea.   He screamed
With horror, shuddered, wailed with piteous cry,
As the giant grim his bony hand stretched forth,
And clutching tight with firm, determined grip,
Bound him in heavy chains of black despair,
And bore away adown the aisle unto—
Then closed the doors;—I saw him ne'er again.
"The atheist meets the atheist's doom," said I

Unto myself, revolving in my mind

This scene so wonderful and strange.—But while

I mused and pondered thus, re-entered DEATH;

And silent still he marched along.　But, oh!

How changed! Not now, as black, terrific as

The thunder-cloud his face!　Was figure of

A mortal man or supernatural being

E'er altered so?　But to describe I'll not

Attempt.　To say that terror, anger, fear,

And gloom had disappeared must now suffice;

While e'en turned white that banner was, afore

As black as Erebus itself; and that

Strange motto too, in characters subdued,

To view shone forth, and a bright wreath of light

Was thrown around like interwoven, clustering

Rays of gleaming hope.

　　　　　　　　And with a countenance

So changed approached he then to where a weak,

And silent sufferer lay—a woman wan,

On whose face pale, as Parian marble white,

Calmness and resignation sat.   But bright
And radiant 'twas as holy angels' fair.
And with a glowing smile of ecstasy
And rapture most intense, DEATH greeted she;
Aud hailed him glad as her deliverer from
All earthly woes and pains, afflictions hard.
He bore her willing down that avenue;
And oped the doors, and shut.

     "The righteous fear
Not DEATH," thought I, and wondered if he would
Return and bear off to the grave still yet
Another one of these whom pale Disease
Had prostrate thrown upon their beds of trial
And suffering.

     Yes, re-entered he again;
But more this time like to some fair spirit bright,
From Heaven high, than being from the realms
Of Hell, as he had first to me appeared!
And noiselessly he walked along, until
He came unto a little cot where I

Saw on a pillow soft a rosebud white,

Not e'en half-blown, whose once fair, ruby cheek

The frost had touched, and nipped its bloom.   Withered

It lay—its blush now gone—to pine, decay.

Gently as e'en a mother fond her child

Would to her heaving, feeling, yearning breast

Clasp in the arms of love, the tiny flower

He pressed unto his bosom warm, and walked

Away, to bear the fair exotic frail

And tender—chilled thus, ere its perfect bloom,

By frosty breath of wan Disease—from this

Cold, gloomy, foreign land;—to bear off this

Poor, blighted bud unto the sunny clime whence

First it came, to grow, expand, and cast its

Smiles and fragrance 'neath bright Heaven's genial light!

And now three thus borne off had he—a man,

A woman, babe—an infidel who scoffed,

And cursed his God, and greatly feared to die—

And next a woman, who, tired of this life,

Was glad to go unto a land wherein
Lived pain and sorrow not—and last this sweet
And beauteous babe, in mercy carried from
A suffering world to one of happiness,
And joy, and love.

               I woke—'twas but a dream,
Yet not without a moral, lesson, fraught;
Which was just this, summed up in but few words—
That pleasant Death appears, and kind, and mild,
Or dread, terrific, awful, dark, e'er as
The preparation is of mind and heart
To leave this for another world—to die!

ODE TO

N. P. WILLIS, Esq.

Hail! Poet-author, hail! to thee
Upon whose manly brow we see
A sparkling crown with glowing gem,
As bright as e'en the diadem
   Of "ebon goddess" Night,
   Lit with the lamps of light!

Hail! Poet-author, hail! to thee; —
Thy winged thoughts have crossed the sea, —
That others save thy countrymen
May see and catch and hold them then—
   And there been caged in heart
   Of man, ne'er to depart.

And thy "Home Journal" e'er is found
To send delight and pleasure round
The hearth-stone glad.   Oh! may it e'er
Wave pure as Truth's white banner dear,
  While thoughts shine there like star
  In the milky-way afar!

To Mrs. A. C.

Be thy heart e'er as light,
And thy smiles softly bright,
As are these sweet flowers
From kind Nature's rich bowers—
Is a prayer I would make
For old friendship's dear sake.
And may hope's buds as sweet,
Ever lie at thy feet,
'Long thy pathway through life,
Mellowing sorrow and strife! —
When these short years are o'er,
On the green, sunny shore

Of that cool sparkling stream,
 Whose diamond-like gleam
Is the reflection bright
Of God's glorious light—
Of that River of Life,
 Far from sorrow and strife,
May'st thou bloom, a sweet flower,
Not like earth's, of an hour,
But a bright *immortelle,*
There e'er fadeless to dwell!

To Mrs. T. E.

A merry heart maketh a cheerful countenance.
PROV. OF SOLOMON.

LADY fair,
'Tis my prayer
That each new budding hope,
Which e'er within thy heart may grow,
Shall, quick expand and ope,
Real, beauteous flower to love and know,
'Neath Fortune's warm and genial smile,
Free from hypocrisy and guile,
To gladden thee and thine the while,

Until succeeded by
Still others, all as rich and bright
  As stars in azure sky,
Which gild the diadem of Night—
Ne'er nipped by disappointment's frost,
Ne'er by a storm of passion tossed,
As oft an earthly flower is lost,
  When, chilled by Winter's breath,
Or blown before the wild wind's rush,
  It meets a violent death—
Too early loses bloom and blush!

  Lady fair,
    'Tis my prayer
That thy face happy, bright,
As if it always did reflect
  The sun's mild, genial light,
May ever thus be sweetly decked
With Joy's warm smiles so rich so gay,
E'er gladdening with their golden ray
Those who with thee a moment stay!

Thus may it ever be,
Telling of thy heart's happiness,
So cheerful, light, and free;
Unchilled by wing of pale Distress;
Ne'er darkened by a cloud e'en small,
Or great to hang like a funeral pall,
Which might in gloom wrap pleasures all.

But should Misfortune's frown
Cast over thee her shadow drear,
To earth be not cast down
But e'er upheld by Faith's hand dear!

TO MISS C. W.

My Artist-friend, hail, now!
To thee my muse would bow
In honor; for, though still so young,
Genius' flames in thy breast have sprung.—
  'Tis said Prometheus bold,
  When Jove mad did withhold

  Heaven's bright fire from man,
  By some ingenious plan
Stole rays of light from the chariot strong
Of Sol as swift it whirled along;
  And that these power possessed,
  When placed within the breast

Of statues which he cut,
To make them live and strut!
Such vital spark hath Genius placed
Within thy bosom illumined, graced.
Oh! let its blaze die ne'er,
But cherish it fore'er,

As Vestal Virgins white
Watched flames both day and night
Upon the sacred altar which
Burned for their goddess, bright and rich,
Year after year the same,
As past it went and came.

Let it e'er glow and smile;—
Oh! smother not with pile
Of velvets, satins, silks, heaped high!
Beware, lest it should flicker, die,
In fashion's whirlwind blown,
Thy soul in darkness thrown!

THE STAR OF DESTINY.

Bonaparte used to say this star made its appearance at the hour of his birth, and that by consulting it he could always tell when good fortune awaited him; for that, then, it glowed with unusual brightness; but grew pallid and hueless when defeat or disaster was about to befall him.

BOTTA.

NEAR Italia's classic shore there lies a sunny isle—

   Golden beauty-spot on Ocean's bosom fair!

Glowing in its loveliness 'neath Heaven's radiant smile.

   But for man's sad fall angels might pause there!

Where the breath of blossoms of tropic trees and flowers,

To God as incense rises from Nature's vine-clad bowers;

And the joyous songs of birds of golden plumage bright,

   As anthems pour, till eve from early morn.

Oh! how the heart rejoices moved by the glorious sight!

   'Twas here a child of fortune strange was born—

In this tropic sunlit isle—a fairy ocean gem,

The richest, brightest jewel in France's diadem!

In a lone, secluded spot,
Is a shaded, hidden grot,
Which, from Nature's chisel sprung,
Is with ivy curtains hung;
Whose rough walls strange shadows strow,
Moving ghost-like to and fro,
Spirits-like in play or dance,
Sometimes seen by the eye in trance—
Dim reflections from the mind
Of a youth whom there we find,
Wrapt in vision's mantle gray,
Dreaming thus whole hours away!
Rolls a canvas past his eyes,
Gilt with scenes of various dyes.

First he sees a chariot bring
In great pomp a mighty king
To a throne o'erlaid with gold,
Guarded by his soldiers bold.
But, hark! now, what thundering sound,
Like an earthquake shakes the ground?

Soon a multitude draws near,
Crying loud with curse and jeer:
" Vengeance! now, the king shall die!
No longer will his subjects lie,
Trod beneath his charger's heel,
Crushed beneath the ponderous wheel
Of his great triumphal car
Rolling to and fro to mar,
With its deep and bloody trace,
Our dear country's once fair face!
Like the march of Juggernaut,
All its way with death is fraught!
Royalty shall fall, the nest
Whence brood woes that tear our breast! "

Next he sees a mighty crowd
Gesturing wild, and threatening loud,
Pressing round a trembling band
Clasping each another's hand.
Heaven reflected in the eye,
Surely they fear not to die!

Soon an instrument of death

Draws their blood and stops their breath!

And a stream of *royal* blood,

Dyes the ground with purple flood,

In which Law's strong ark sinks down!

Anarchy assumes the crown.

Midnight darkness drives off day.

Sickened thus he turns away,

Nothing bright save one lone star

Gleaming in the distance far,

Shining 'mid universal gloom,—-

Dark and dreary as a tomb—

Like a sparkling jewel set,

In enamel black as jet!—

Wonders why, when all is dark

It alone should cast a spark.

And unconscious where he goes,

Still his eye he upward throws,

Held enchanted by that light

Frowned upon by gloomy Night!—

Strolls along through street and lane,
'Till he sees no blood of slain—
Reaches now a shady grove,
Far from where Hell's demons strove!
Here a fairy-form he spies.
Can he trust his weary eyes?
Yes, a creature bright draws near,
With a smile dispelling fear,
While a wreath of snowflakes white
On her brow throws out its light;
And a cloud of rainbow hues,
Spangled o'er with diamond dews,
Wraps her form in mystery's robe,
As in hand she holds a globe.
She approaching takes his hand,
Addressing thus in manner bland:

"Hail! Child of Fortune, hark to me;
    List to the words I tell,
And thou shalt yet a monarch be,
    And in a palace dwell!

"Dost see that light through yonder tree—
    Lone hope of brighter day?
It is thy star of destiny—
    Trust in its guiding ray.

"Behold this globe turn 'neath my finger;
    Thus thou shalt move the earth!
But farewell now, I cannot linger—
    Hear! France will bless thy birth!"

He awakes—'tis but a dream,
Yet distinct with dazzling gleam,—
Sees those shadows come and go,
Moving ghost-like to and fro—
Like spirits in the play or dance,
Sometimes seen by the eye in trance—,
Dim reflections from the mind
Of this youth, who there doth find
Study for another hour,
Thinking of his future power,

Saying as he claps in glee,
"I shall yet a monarch be!"

Oft he dreamed, and dreamed of fame—
Of a great and glorious name—
Of a throne of crowns built high,
'Neath the canopy of sky,
Curtained by the drooping cloud
Of imperial purple proud!
Thus he hoped and dreamed a child,
Clinging to his fancies wild.
When to man's estate he came,
Still he hoped and dreamed the same.

Long strange Fortune with her ear,
Through the heavens drew his star.
Now that guiding star was bright;
Then it almost sank in night!
Oft its golden rays would shed,
A halo-glory round his head,

And then throw a shadow foul
Round his brow, black as a cowl!
Now in zenith of the skies,
Its bright light would blind all eyes;
Then to the horizon near,
There it trembled as with fear!

When on Elba's shore he lay,
Like a lion but held at bay,
It a faithful sentinel
Stood and watched its hero well.
When to France again he went,
Shone that star on him intent—
Bright again in his success—
Pale again in his distress!

When old Waterloo was fought,
All the ground with dying fraught,
Cannons belching forth fire fell,—
Like the demons mad of Hell'—

Wrapping troops in shrouds of smoke,
From which thousands never broke,—
Flames and smoke wild running fast,
Breathing death where'er they passed,
Like Vesuvius in his rage,
Heedless both of youth and age;
Hurling forth each red-hot wave,
Sent all beneath his head to lave,
Flapping each forked tongue of fire,
As if thus 'twould spit its ire;
Lapping up all sap of life,
In mad rush and war and strife;—
When old Waterloo was done,
And from earth was hid the sun,
And it seemed to be now night,
Though no moon was there to light,
With its soft and silver sheen,
This terrible, and awful scene—
Battle-ground too dread to see,
Where in blood and agony

Piles of human beings lay,
Waning life, or gone away; —
Then that star almost went down,
'Neath wild Terror's fearful frown!
When to ocean's rock firm chained.
While dark gloom around him reigned;
Watched close by the keen, fierce eye
Of the British Lion e'er nigh;
At the mercy of his foes,
He stood suffering cruel woes,
Such as mortals seldom feel,—
Pains ne'er made by piercing steel,
Helpless as Andromeda,
Who, the olden poets say,
Fastened to the sea-beat wall,
Filled the air with mercy's call,
When the dragon's look so fierce,
Like a dart her breast would pierce: —
When his wrestle with Death, long
As Jacob's with the angel strong,

Like an earthquake shook the world.
Then that trembling star was hurled
From its station, and its light,
Quenched in black and endless night!

AN ODE TO

ALFRED TENNYSON, Esq.

THE Romans old,
The Romans bold,
Long dead,
'Tis said
To grace
Would place,
In state,
Pomp great,
A wreath—
Beneath
A gaily gilded, lofty arch,
O'er his proud, grand triumphal march—
Of laurel green upon the head
Of a loved victor, who had lead

Them on to glory
O'er war's fields gory.
Poet Laureate,
In pomp and state
A grateful nation decks thy brow
With a bright crown of glory now!

Old Ovid dead
With pride once said
That he had finished a work grand
Which e'er would fire, sword, age withstand!
Indelible his name through time;
Nor e'en Jove's wrath mar it sublime!—
Thy *In Memoriam* shall stand,
A monument that Time's strong hand
Shall not pull down while our great tongue
Can still be heard the nations 'mong!
And many a turret, many a spire,
That round about with beauty grace
This noble, lofty shaft, their place
Shall hold despite of sword and fire!

The Poetical Salmagundi.

PLUCK NOW THE FLOWER.

Τὸ ῥόδον ἀκμάζει βαιὸν χρόνον ἢν δὲ παρέλθῃ,
Ζητῶν εὑρήσεις οὐ ῥόδον ἀλλὰ βατόν.

O MAN, do not procrastinate;
Pluck now the flower before too late.
Do not neglect the chance, and say:
"Not now, I'll come again this way;"—
Perhaps no living, earthly power
'Till then can keep that smiling flower;
And when again thou dost go there
Thou may'st not find that blossom fair.

It may be withered, fallen, dead,
And in the dust have sunk its head.
Perchance thou 'lt find another one,
Passing that way, the thing hath done
Thou did'st neglect, in thy weak ear
Procrastination whispering, " Here,
Man, do not stop, 'tis useless now,—
To-morrow cull that flower canst thou."

A TRANSLATION FROM HORACE.

ODE XXX. BOOK III.

THE POET'S PRESAGE OF AN IMMORTALITY OF FAME.

I 'VE built a monument more lasting far than brass,
Which doth the regal hight of pyramids surpass;
'Gainst which nor wasting rains, nor north-wind, can avail,
Nor years, nor seasons' flight leave ruined in their trail.
I shall not wholly die; but a great part of me,
From Libitina dark escaping, then shall flee.
My name with future praise posterity shall blend,
While priest and vestal maid the capitol ascend.

Where rapid Aufidus in violent flight doth roar—
Where Dannus, poor supplied with water, ruleth o'er
A rustic people, I, raised from a low degree,
Shall be forever there acknowledged him to be,
Who did the first of all arrange and make to meet
The old Æolic verse, and the Italian feet.
Melpomene, assume that pride for you meet seen,
And willing crown my hair with Delphic laurel green.

TO

POLLIE ANN JELICA(KE).

O, FAIR one, thou

Of the angel brow,

By whom alone my heart is whirled,

You 've the prettiest eye in all the world,

And the sweetest lip that e'er was curled.

Kinder heart never beat;

Not oft can one meet

Disposition so sweet,

As ever is thine.

Fair creature, divine!

No man with thee would fear earth's strife!

Thy soul with sympathy so rife—

Oh! say, bright star of my whole life,

Say, wont you be, from this, my ——!

The remainder of this beautiful and exciting poem will be concluded in the great NEW JERUSALEM BLUNDERBUSS, published weekly, and to be found in all the literary depots in America, Europe, Asia, Africa, and the other extensive hemispheres of the world, whose price is five cents per one copy, ten cents per two copies, and so on *ad infinitum*, to the end of this sublunary globe. A more *liberal discount still* made to the wholesale trade!! Don't forget! Send one, send all!

BIDDY AND PAT.

Biddy O'Connell
And Pat O'Donnell
Sat 'neath an old elm on the bank of a brook.
Quoth Pat to fair Biddy: "An' sure an' ye look
Intirely as swate as yon rose in its nook,
As cunningly now ye pape from that gray
Hood ye have on, an' *hood-wink* at the day,
With sich chareful face, an' so bright, an' so gay."
"Och! murther! mon, hush! ye have towld me enough
Ye might as well ram in me ears so much snuff.
Your story is as your big hand as tough!

An' sure, crazy loon! now, what if I do
Look as swate as the rose; an' what 's that to you
I swear be me *sowl* ye will *niver* be true!"

"Oh! Biddy, me darlin', I kinnot stand that;
I love ye much more than this me owld hat.
Indade, don't your heart bid ye pity Pat?"

"Och! yis, to be sure, swate, pilavering brat,
I, be the howly beard of St. Pathrick, swear that
Me heart oll the time repates *pit-a-pat!*"

"POSSUNT QUIA POSSE VIDENTUR."

VIRGIL.

"FOR THEY CAN CONQUER WHO BELIEVE THEY CAN."

DRYDEN.

O, Faith and Will are giants strong;
'Twas they who threw the Alps headlong,
And made them level with the ground,
As down they fell with crashing sound,
That Hannibal with troops might rush
On Italy, as torrents gush
When, swollen by the April rain,
They raging their bold course maintain,—
In spite of all that may withstand
O'erflowing all the fertile land.

'Twas Faith and Will that guided o'er
The Mayflower to the Western shore;
And then from barbarism wild
Redeemed a continent, which smiled
Quite soon with peace and plenty fraught,
Beneath their wholesome sway thus brought;—
And when 'twas necessary broke
The galling, binding foreign yoke
Which had been let thereon to fall,
And press it like a massive wall.

And Faith and Will the chasm deep
'Tween Earth and Heaven, where there e'er sweep
Black waters raging wild, have bridged
So that tired pilgrims, privileged,
May pass from this dark, mournful clime
Up to that golden land sublime!

Since Faith and Will can do so much,
Oh! try to know them—genii such.

A LOVE–MESS–AGE.

RESPECTFULLY INSCRIBED TO

MISS MERCY ELIZABETH SAMUELINA SNAGWALLADER.

ESAU has been pronounced a fool
By all the wise and sapient school
Of great philosophers, smart men,
Who think it is past mortal ken,
That for a single mess he'd give
All that for which most men do live.
Should I be thought a fool the less,
Who 'd give my all for a *single M. E. S. S!*

"ΦΕΙΔΕΩ ΤΩΝ ΚΤΕΑΝΩΝ."

"TAKE CARE OF THY POSSESSIONS."

Epigram Vet.

LIST, spendthrift, to the precept taught,
Ere·in poverty's tight net caught ;
Whence thou mayst never make escape
In any form, disguise, or shape ;
For prodigality is sure
A very hard disease to cure,—
A rapid stream running so fast
That it is hard to check at last;
And in thy nature flowing deep
It rushes on with awful sweep.

The maxim doth not mean to say,
That thou shouldst hoard thy goods away,
As e'en the miser his doth hold,
Making of all a seat of gold,
So that he can 'neath him at once
Keep all his " filthy lucre,"—dunce !—
Fearing that it might melt and go
Quicker than ever it did flow
In golden streams his coffers to ; —
It does not bid thee thus to do ;
But husband well what thou dost gain,
Lest thy possessions be a bane ;
Use for thyself what thou shouldst need,
Neglecting not the kind, good deed.

26

AN EXAMPLE OF ALLITERATION,

Simpletons sometimes show sense, smart speeches say:
Think to-morrow they'd talk thus, though thus to-day?
Gabbling geese garrulous gained great, glorious gratitude,
Renown, rousing regardless Rome reposing, rude
Barbarian bands being but beheld before
They through those thousand thoroughfares, thronging tore!
Thence twenty times these thoughtless things threw terror
    thus,
May be, 'mong mighty men, meaninglessly making muss!

A COLLEGE SONG.

Diamond and bright, as the stars of night,
　　Is our joy and glee now glowing,
And the gay smile, so free from all guile,
　　Its radiance brightly flowing.

CHORUS.

Then sing how grand, ye merry band,
　　Linonia in her glory,
Whose walls so high, arched by the sky,
　　Excel all ancient story!

A few more years, with their joys and cares,
We'll rest 'neath Yale's elms spreading;
Then world's broad stage our acts will engage,
As the sands of time we're treading.

CHORUS.

Then thy deeds grand, ye victor band,
Write now on Fame's tall pillar;
While these walls high, arched by the sky,
Defy time's angry billow!

And should drear clouds overhang like shrouds,
And our craft be sadly reeling,
We'll safe be then, for our guiding star
Will glow, our path revealing.

CHORUS.

Then sing how grand, ye noble band,
The stage our thought engages,
Whose walls so strong will stand as long,
As time's firm rock of ages!

Through battles strong, we will fight along,
  Above our bright star flashing;
And coats of mail, the memory of Yale,
  As we are forward dashing.

CHORUS.

Then bravely sing, ye gallant ring,
  Of armies once before us;
When our walls high did all defy,
  As Victory hovered o'er us!

Yale College, 1855.

AN ALBUMIC.

TO MY BIG BROTHER'S LITTLE SWEETHEART.

> Vanity of vanities—all is vanity.
>> ECCLES. I.
>
> Flatterie is unwholesome foode for younge ladyes.
>> OLD ENGLISH AUTHOR.

An album is—don't box my phiz—
　A cunning flattery-trap well set,
Fine compliments from gallant gents,
　And "sweet, nice things" to get!

I mean to say that that's the way
　The thing in general is—but oh!
Thou wouldst not act with such mean tact—
　No, never condescend so low.

And men too oft will pen words soft—
   Write love not felt, O shame!—but then
Thou know'st that I would rather die
   Than *flatter* thee—*the truth I pen!*

Your quick, keen eye, like a star on high
   Illumines with its rays my soul!
That mirror bright with Heaven's own light
   Reflects your thoughts as on they roll!

Expressive nose!—indeed it throws
   The Roman, Carthaginian, Greek,
All in the shade, nor e'en art's aid
   A nose can give, that thus can speak!

That mouth of thine! O, how divine!
   It is a perfect Cupid's bow;
Indeed if he could but thine see,
   I know his own away he'd throw!

Those teeth, O my!—in earth or sky,
　　To what can I those teeth compare?
To pearls, snow-flakes?—indeed it takes
　　To match them something else more rare!

Thy sunny smile, so free from guile,
　　An angel would not blush to wear!
Within its light, from morn till night,
　　Pain, woe, and torment I could bear!

Those tresses now fall on thy brow,
　　Like moonbeams on a marble bust!
Their light o'erspread forms round thy head
　　A halo-glory, rich, august!

And then that voice, O, I rejoice
　　To hear it ring like silver bells!
The syren, no! nor swan of snow
　　Could dying match its magic swells!

And now, fair one, before I 'm done,
　I do not mean to *flatter* thee,
No rival thou cast have I vow;
　E'en angels can but equal bo!

OLD CANNIBAL VI.

THE world has had equals to bold Hannibal,
But where, when a match for the great cannibal
Old Virgil speaks of when, *bona fide*, he'd say,
Vi eat armies?—Vi eat armies!—indeed! nay,
Can it be possible?—can such thing be true?
But then we must believe, for it never would do—
'Twould show a sad want of prudence, sagacity—
To question, the least, old Virgil's veracity.
But Vi's great *voracity*, oh! who can doubt,
As he swallowing armies thus put them in rout,—

En route for a singular, strange destiny,

Which, doubtless, these legions did never foresee.

Nine *cheeries*, three *tigers*, ten men for old Vi;

And an elephant too, for all earth we defy

King Vi to out-*vie* in the great *causa belly !*

For he was a glutton colossal, I tell ye.

E'en Old Polyphemus the giant Cyclops,

Who in his tremendous and mastodon chops,

Which worked up and down like the parts of a trunk,

And at each clap a man of Ulysses' sunk,—

Where boys studying German could begin to do learning—

Schul' welch' ich erachte nicht schlecht deutsch zu lernen—

Where with ease they could catch the deep *guttural* sound—

Here, in this resounding, deep school most profound—

Such school as that wherein old Jonah was taught

The most memorable lesson that ever was bought

With the "wages of sin," though indeed it was cheap,

Paying naught to his *sea*-lord the king of the deep,

For being *boarded* thus in his *craft* and so *taken in,*

While opening deceitful mouth with a broad grin !—

Yes, e'en Polyphemus, the giant Cyclops,

Who, in his tremendous and mastodon chops,

Chopped up these poor men into fine sausage-meat,

Holding this motto, "it is *meat* I should eat,"

And not being particular as to the kind,

Flesh and blood swallowing where'er he could find—

Why he wasn't a mite to our *mighty* king Vi,

Who ne'er went to buy, stealing those who *went by*.

What *vis*-count, now, could with our Vi count such kind

Of deeds done in the body, although, *never mind* ——

VALEDICTION.

Gentle reader and friend,
This volume must end ;
My thoughts all poetical having *run down*,
To *wind up* it's time,
And thus close my rhyme.—
You'll doubtless agree without murmur or frown !—

Hold on !—one request,
While I *put on my best*.
And 'tis that this volume you never will lend
Unto an acquaintance, or even a friend,

While a copy's unbought;—
Felicitous thought!—
But send to the store each to buy for one's-self,
Lest long my poor brains may be *laid on the shelf!*
For I this proposition self-evident hold,
That I, or my book, one must surely be *sold.*
Well then let me now be con*soled* for my toil—
Paid for my mind's engine—its *midnight-train-oil!*

716